Praise for
the Blood Coven Vampire Novels

Stake That

"A fast-paced story line . . . both humorous and hip . . . A top read!"
—*Love Vampires*

"Rayne is a fascinating protagonist . . . readers will want to stake out Mari Mancusi's fun homage to Buffy."
—*The Best Reviews*

Boys That Bite

"A wonderfully original blend of vampire/love/adventure drama which teens will find refreshingly different."
—*Midwest Book Review*

"Liberal doses of humor keep things interesting . . . and the surprise ending will leave readers bloodthirsty for the next installment of the twins' misadventures with the undead. A ghoulishly fun read."
—*School Library Journal*

"A tongue-in-cheek young-teen tale starring two distinct, likable twins, the vampire between them, and a coven of terrific support characters who bring humor and suspense to the mix . . . [F]illed with humor and action . . . insightfully fun."
—*The Best Reviews*

GIRLS THAT GROWL

MARI MANCUSI

BERKLEY JAM, NEW YORK

THE BERKLEY PUBLISHING GROUP
Published by the Penguin Group
Penguin Group (USA) Inc.
375 Hudson Street, New York, New York 10014, USA
Penguin Group (Canada), 90 Eglinton Avenue East, Suite 700, Toronto, Ontario M4P 2Y3, Canada
(a division of Pearson Penguin Canada Inc.)
Penguin Books Ltd., 80 Strand, London WC2R 0RL, England
Penguin Group Ireland, 25 St. Stephen's Green, Dublin 2, Ireland (a division of Penguin Books Ltd.)
Penguin Group (Australia), 250 Camberwell Road, Camberwell, Victoria 3124, Australia
(a division of Pearson Australia Group Pty. Ltd.)
Penguin Books India Pvt. Ltd., 11 Community Centre, Panchsheel Park, New Delhi—110 017, India
Penguin Group (NZ), 67 Apollo Drive, Rosedale, North Shore 0632, New Zealand
(a division of Pearson New Zealand Ltd.)
Penguin Books (South Africa) (Pty.) Ltd., 24 Sturdee Avenue, Rosebank, Johannesburg 2196,
South Africa

Penguin Books Ltd., Registered Offices: 80 Strand, London WC2R 0RL, England

Copyright © 2007 by Marianne Mancusi.
Cover art by Shutterstock.
Cover design by SDG Concepts, LLC.
Text design by Tiffany Estreicher.

PRINTING HISTORY
Berkley JAM trade paperback edition / October 2007

Library of Congress Cataloging-in-Publication Data

Mancusi, Marianne.
   Girls that growl / Mari Mancusi.—Berkeley Jam trade paperback ed.
      p. cm.
   Summary: Rayne McDonald, a goth vampire and vampire slayer, must go undercover as a cheerleader at her high school to find out what happened to the captain of the football team, who has disappeared, and to see if the peppy cheerleaders are really werewolves.
   ISBN 978-0-425-21716-0
   [1. Vampires—Fiction. 2. Goth culture (Subculture)—Fiction. 3. Werewolves—Fiction. 4. Cheerleading—Fiction. 5. Twins—Fiction. 6. Sisters—Fiction. 7. High schools—Fiction. 8. Schools—Fiction.] I. Title.

PZ7.M312178Gi 2007
[Fic]—dc22
                                    200702356

PRINTED IN THE UNITED STATES OF AMERICA

15 14 13 12 11 10 9 8 7

Rayne McDonald
Vampire & Vampire Slayer
8 Peace Lane
St. Patrick's Cemetery
Oakridge, MA
(617) 555–1432
raynieday@yours.com

Mr. Joss Whedon
Producer of *Buffy*, *Angel*, and various other rocking shows
Mutant Enemy Productions
Hollywood, CA

Dear Joss:

How's things in the Whedonverse? Pretty dull, I bet, now that *Buffy* and *Angel* have bitten it and *Firefly*'s flown. Yeah, I'd be willing to guess you're just sitting around, twiddling your thumbs, dying to find the perfect project to sink your teeth into, right?

Well, Joss, look no further! Have I got a project for you! This would make an *excellent* TV show. Or even a movie. Or hey, why not both? (In case they bury the series on Friday nights and we end up having to push some DVDs.) It's got vampires and vampire slayers and best of all, it's absolutely true!

My name is Rayne McDonald and last year I signed up to become a vampire. I got myself on the waiting list, took my Vamp Certification class, etc., etc. But then, the night I was supposed to be transformed into a creature of the night, this idiot vampire assigned to be my blood mate made a huge mistake and bit my identical twin sister, Sunshine, instead. (Yes, Sunshine and Rayne. Think of all the joke potential in our names alone, Joss!)

Anyway, at the time, Sunny had no idea vampires even existed (sad to say she's not a *Buffy* fan either) and she was so not happy to find out she was now morphing into one against her will. So she teamed up with the hottie vampire who bit her (Magnus, current master of our local coven) and the two of them managed to find the Holy Grail (!!) and remortalize her just in time for the prom. In the meantime, Sunny and Magnus fell in love and are presently doing the interspecies dating thing. (Think Buffy and Angel, though I'm guessing they can get it on without him going all evil and destroying the world. But since my sister is still a virgin, one never knows for sure . . .)

Good stuff, huh? But hold on to your pop culture clichés, Joss, it gets even better. The next week, this crazy antivampire company called Slayer Inc. suddenly informed me that I'm their new vampire slayer! Me! The girl voted most likely to become a blood sucker is now supposed to slay them for a living. (Not that they pay me. Grr.) I tried to refuse, of course, but they insisted it's my destiny and threatened to kill me with some crazy nanovirus if I didn't take the gig. So what choice did I have, right?

So, during my first assignment—to kill an evil vamp who is manufacturing a blood disease that would weaken the vampire population and allow him to take over as master—I hook up with this uber-hot goth vampire Jareth. At first I don't like the guy much, but eventually he grows on me. You know, like Spike does with Buffy. (Except Jareth didn't go and withstand trials and torture to redeem his lost soul like Spike did for the Buffster. Do you think I should have held out for that?)

In any case, together, Jareth and I were able to take down the Big Bad, as Buffy would say, and save the vampire world as we know it. Problem is, before we did, Maverick managed to infect me with the virus. To save my life, Jareth bit me and turned me into a vampire. By doing so, he also became infected.

So now the two of us are essentially gimped vampires. We don't have superstrength, or superhearing, or super *anything*, really (well, besides my superGoth fashion sense, which I must admit is pretty darn super), but we do have some advantages. Unlike other vampires, we can go out during the day. And that makes us extremely valuable to the vampire community. (And great for a hit show on the CW!)

As for Slayer Inc., they figured that having an actual vampire on the payroll could bring down their corporate image, so they put me on disability and started training the next girl. I still technically work for them freelance until the new Slayer is fully trained. But hopefully there won't be any actual assignments. After all, I'm entering junior year in high school. I've got a hot new boyfriend. And I'm finally a member of the Blood Coven. Yay me!

So tell me, does this not sound like a series that will rock the socks of every teen in America? Come on, Joss. You know you want to become part of the Raynieverse.

Love,
Rayne McDonald
Vampire & Vampire Slayer

1

"So, should I or shouldn't I?"

I groan and throw myself back on my bed. "Sunny, it's not something I can tell you either way. You have to decide for yourself whether or not you're ready."

"But you've been there. Done that."

"Yes, and I have the 'I lost my virginity to a skanky skater kid at camp' T-shirt. What of it?" I don't mean to sound flip, but this isn't the first time we've had this conversation. Now that I think about it, this isn't the tenth time either. And every time she brings it up, I say the same thing. Having sex for the first time is a personal decision no one can make but you.

"I'm not joking," Sunny protests, rummaging through my closet. As if she'd actually wear any of the striped tights, lacy skirts, or delicate corsets I've stocked it with. We may be identical twins, but she's strictly a jeans, tank, and flips kind of girl, even if her boyfriend is a vampire coven master. Not that Magnus would win Mr. Goth himself. Which, in my opinion, is such a waste. Why be a vampire if you aren't going to take advantage of the basic wardrobe?

"Is Magnus pressuring you?" I ask, trying a new tactic. So help him if he's dicking my sister around. (Or trying to, as the case may be.) Powerful vampire master or no, I'll totally find a way to kick his scrawny English ass. "Like, is he saying he'll break up with you if you don't put out?" Needless to say, I've heard that line before. Stupid guys!

"No, no!" Sunny says, sounding shocked at the idea. Of course. In her mind, Maggy Waggy walks on water and saves the world before breakfast. "He's been great. Patient. Supportive. He's left it totally up to me."

"So that should make it easy."

"Yeah, right."

"Sunny, come here." I motion to the bed. She leaves the closet and approaches me. "Sit down. Look me in the eyes and answer this question: Do you or do you not want to have sex with Magnus?"

Sunny flops back on the bed with an agonizing groan. "Can't we call it 'making love' or something? I mean, 'sex' sounds so clinical."

I dig my fingernails into my palms, wondering how I can run screaming from the room without offending her too much. I so don't want to be having this conversation.

"Sure, whatever, call it what you want, Sun," I force myself to say brightly. "Making love, screwing, doing the wild thing, hooking up, getting it on. It really doesn't matter what you want to refer to it as. Just if you feel you're ready. And if you want to."

"I want to," Sunny whines. "But I'm scared."

Okay, that's it. I've made the decision for her. "Fine. Then maybe you should wait. I mean, if you're this conflicted . . ."

"But I love Magnus!"

How many years in jail do you think I'll get for killing my sister?

"Then do it. Or don't. I don't care. I don't even get why you're asking me anyway. You don't listen to anything I have to say!" I jump off the bed and head to my computer, loading up iTunes, ready to drown out anymore conversation.

Okay, fine, I probably sound like the worst twin sister known to mankind, but you'd be losing patience, too, if you had to have this conversation twenty times in one week. Especially if the other nineteen times you tried to impart wise, sisterly advice and she never listened to a word of it. At the end of the day, she's going to do whatever she decides to do. Hashing it out with me is only time suckage.

Sunny sticks out her lower lip in a pout. "Fine," she says. "Don't help me."

I turn from the computer, my finger still hovering on the PLAY button. "Sunny, if you don't stop this, I'm going to strangle you to death. And then you won't have a decision to make."

My twin opens her mouth to speak, but luckily at that moment the front door creaks open. Mom must be home. Time for all talk of sex to cease.

We head downstairs to greet her. She's got her arms full of groceries from the local Harvest Co-Op. I take a paper bag from her and bring it into the kitchen. Sunny heads to the car to grab what's left.

"Thanks," Mom says as we put the groceries in the cabinets and fridge. I grimace as I pull out some kind of purple, crinkly vegetable I don't recognize.

"What is—?"

Mom shrugs. "I don't know exactly. But it was on sale."

Typical. Mom's an ex-hippie who used to live in an actual commune in upstate New York before my dad whisked her away and impregnated her with twins. She may be all soccer mom wannabe now, but her kitchen remains in the Age of

Aquarius. If you can add tofu to a recipe, you can be sure my mom's done it. Not that it matters much to me anymore. As a vampire, I can't eat. Which is a relief, when it comes to Mom's cooking.

"So girls, I have something I need to talk to you about," Mom says, sitting down at the table after the groceries are put away. "It's about David."

David is Mom's boyfriend. Last spring we thought he was an evil vampire and tried to douse him with a Super Soaker amount of holy water. Turns out, he's actually a guardian for Slayer Inc., the company I've been working for. He fell in love with my mom while on assignment to watch over me. They've been dating all summer. He's okay, I guess. But kind of geeky and out there. Which makes him a good match for Mom, but annoying to be around at times. Luckily, he lives across town.

"He's going to be living here."

What? I look at Sunny and then back at my mom.

"Live here?" Sunny asks, sounding as incredulous as I feel.

"He's moving in? He can't move in! You barely know the guy."

Mom frowns. "Rayne, I will decide that, not you. And besides, it's only temporary. He's having his condo renovated and he needs a place to stay."

"No way!" I protest. "This house is a Girl's Only Zone. I mean, there are tampons in the bathroom cabinet. My bras are hanging from the shower curtain rod."

"Maybe this will encourage you to pick up after yourselves once in a while," Mom counters.

I decide to switch tactics, to avoid being hammered by a clean-up-your-room lecture on top of everything else. "Mom, what kind of moral lesson does this send to your daughters? Shacking up with some random guy!" I feign horror.

"Why, you're right, Rayne!" Sunny says, catching on. "Maybe I should see if my boyfriend wants to move in with me. After all, we've been dating at least a month longer than Mom and David."

Mom rolls her eyes. "Give me a break, girls," she says, unmoved by our shocked morality. "And besides, he's not staying in my room."

Sunny and I look at one another.

"Uh, where is he staying then? This is a three-bedroom house."

"He'll be staying in one of your rooms," Mom explains in the most matter-of-fact tone, though I can see she's avoiding meeting our eyes. "You'll have to share a room while he's here."

Oh no. No way.

We will just have to see about that.

2

I can't believe it's the first day of school already. Seems like the summer flew by.

Sure, technically I don't *have* to go to school anymore. After all, I'm an immortal vampire. Part of the coven. I could just collapse on a velvet couch and sip blood cocktails from a crystal goblet. But at the same time, if I'm going to live thousands of years, I figure I might as well spend a few finishing high school. Get myself an education. After all, I've met more than a few undead dropouts and they're dreadfully dull at dinner parties.

Not to mention if I want to stay living with Mom and Sunny I've got to keep up the normal teenager act.

Still, as I walk down the halls of Oakridge High, dressed in a black lacy Lolita dress, fishnets, and platform boots, swinging my *Beetlejuice* lunchbox, I wonder if this really was such a good idea. I mean, it's so obvious I don't fit in here with the rest of the Mean Girls and jock boys. I watch them, as if I'm a fly on the wall, as they excitedly greet each other, first-day-of-school style. The trend slaves in their brightly colored, back-to-the-eighties, horizontal striped shirts, belts, and leggings. The retro grunger girls in their shapeless dresses worn over bell-bottom pants. The preps in their skinny jeans and slouchy boots. Everyone has a style that suits their clique. Maybe in a bigger school there'd be others that look like me. Not here though. Oakridge High sucks.

Not that I care. I am who I am. And I don't need three thousand MySpace friends to validate my existence on this planet.

"Ooh, look! It's Freak Girl!"

I do, however, need to be left alone.

I turn around to see which Oakridge Clone is trying to feel better about her own sorry existence by poking fun at mine. My eyes fall on a cluster of cheerleaders staring at me from across the hall. Of course.

Of all the losers at Oakridge High, cheerleaders have to be the worst. With their sickly sweet fake smiles, swishy skirts, and bouncy, sun-kissed (aka highlighted from the muddy brown color they were born with) blond hair, cheerleaders think they're God's gift to high schools. They expect worship from guys, girls, even teachers. And they get it. And if one isn't interested in falling on their knees to kiss their perfectly sculpted asses, they might as well catch leprosy. The cheerleaders will guarantee them social outcast status for the rest of the year.

"Hey, Freak Girl!" calls another cheerleader. They all look alike to me. "I thought vampires couldn't walk around during the day."

I roll my eyes. Of course she has no idea I really AM a vampire. She's making a clever assumption based on the fact I'm not wearing a stitch of pink.

"Of course we can," I retort back. "How else can we sink our teeth into succulent virgins such as yourself— Oh wait! I'm sorry, I must have been thinking of someone else. Someone who *hasn't* banged the whole football team."

The girl's eyes narrow. "You'd better watch yourself, Freak Girl." Yup, that's her oh-so-clever comeback. No denial either, I note.

"Oh yeah?" I grin saucily, sauntering up to their gang with my most confident steps. "How come?"

"Because if you don't, I'll kick your skanky vampire ass."

I let out an overly loud laugh. Gotta let them know I'm not afraid. "You and what army?"

Another cheerleader steps forward. This one I do recognize. Mandy Matterson, my former best friend back in the day. Before she realized that I was nothing but a roadblock in her journey to high school stardom. She's gone through an extreme makeover since we used to hang—inside and out. Now she's blond, beautiful, and oh so bitchy. No wonder she's the current captain of the squad. I can't believe we were once friends.

"You think you're so cool," Mandy sneers, narrowing her eyes. She wouldn't admit to our former friendship if she was being tortured and threatened. "But really, you're just another Oakridge High wannabe."

I squeeze my hands into fists, fury burning through every vein. That's it. I don't care if it's the first day of school. Or that I'm supposed to be keeping a low profile, what with my new undead status and all. I start to dive toward her.

"Rayne!" Someone grabs my arm and yanks me back, just in the nick of time to save Cheerleading Barbie's perfect Ashlee Simpsonesque "after" nose.

I turn around, annoyed. If I was a healthy vamp, no mortal human would have been able to stop me like that. Stupid blood virus. I should start lifting weights.

I realize it's my current best friend, Spider, who's grabbed me. The only person in school who understands me. Which means she should understand my cheerleader rage and let me go.

"It's not worth it," Spider says, not living up to her potential.

"It is *so* worth it." I growl back, glancing over at the three girls, who are staring at me with haughty expressions. As if they really think they can even lay a scratch on my body. Puh-leeze.

"It's the first day of school. You really want to sit in detention the first day of school? I thought we were going to the My Chemical Romance concert tonight."

I sigh. "You're right, I guess. But look at those smug losers," I say, gesturing over to the Barbies. "They deserve to die."

"Believe me, I'm not saying they don't. Just not necessarily before A period," Spider says rationally. "Besides, Mr. Teifert is looking for you."

Mr. Teifert is the school drama teacher and—as only I know—also vice president of Slayer Inc. I wonder why he's looking for me. After all, I'm technically retired from the Slayer biz. The virus made me too weak to perform my duties. But Teifert says once a Slayer, always a Slayer, and you never know when they might need me.

"Great." What fun assignment will he have for me this time? "Okay. I'll see you at lunch."

I watch as Spider turns and walks down the hallway, wondering why no one picks on her. After all, she's not exactly the most normal kid in school either. When she was born, her parents raised her as "gender neutral"—not treating her as a boy or a girl—just a person. She was only allowed to play with gender neutral toys—no Barbies or trucks for Christmas. And she was never put in dresses or allowed to wear baseball caps. The idea behind these avant-garde parenting techniques was that she could choose which gender she preferred when she was old enough to make the decision. But Spider's always been indecisive. She's now sixteen and she still hasn't made up her mind. Her last boyfriend was a drag queen, so I guess she's getting the best of both worlds.

I sneer one last time at the cheerleaders as I walk by, but they've already moved on to the all-important "Does my makeup look all right?" part of their day and so they ignore me. Attention spans of gnats, let me tell you. I walk to the school auditorium's side entrance and push open the heavy metal door. It clangs shut behind me, leaving me in darkness. I always think the stage is spooky when there's no one about. Not that I should be scared of the dark. After all, I'm the most dangerous creature here.

A spotlight illuminates the stage and Teifert, always one for drama—being the drama teacher and all—sits beneath it in a folding chair. Last year the school put on a great production of *Bye Bye Birdie* with Sunny in the starring role. I have to admit, the girl was pretty good.

"What's up, T?" I greet with a casual wave. "How's it hanging?"

He grunts, running a hand through his wild black hair. I don't think he really approves of me, even if last summer I did save the vampire and human races as we know them. I mean, a girl should get some props for that, I think.

"Rayne, we have a problem. And we need your help," he says, without so much as a "Hey, how was your summer?" intro.

Great. And here I thought all I'd have to worry about this semester was calculus.

"Of course you do." I sigh. "What is it this time?"

"Mike Stevens."

"Mike Stevens?" I scowl at the name of my arch nemesis. Lex Luthor to my Superman. Joker to my Batman. Mike Stevens is captain of the football team and officially the biggest dick in the universe. "What about Mike Stevens?"

"He's missing."

"Uh, okay, T," I say. "Let's get something straight here. Mike Stevens missing doesn't necessarily qualify as a problem. I mean, have you met the guy? Some might say a missing Mike Stevens could be the best thing to happen to Oakridge High in a very long time."

"That's not all," Teifert says. "There's also something suddenly very odd about the cheerleaders."

"Odd about the cheerleaders?" I cock my head. See, I knew I should have kicked their butts when I had my chance. "You mean more odd than usual about a group of girls who want to dance and kick up their legs while wearing short skirts in the middle of a New England November?"

"Yes. And Rayne, this is going to sound strange, but . . ."

Strange. Ha! He's talking to a vampire who's also a vampire slayer who spent her spring exposing an evil vampire and keeping him from destroying the world. "Dude, after all I've been through, nothing's going to sound strange. Absolutely nothing in the known universe."

"Very well then. The cheerleaders? They've been heard, uh . . . growling."

Huh. Then again . . . maybe I'm wrong.

"Uh, growling? What do you mean, growling?"

"We're not sure exactly. But we think there's something very odd about their recent behavior. And now with the school's top quarterback missing, well, we feel it's something we need to check into."

"But I'm a vampire slayer, not Jock Detective. What does this have to do with me?"

"Rayne, why is it you feel the need to argue with every single thing I say?"

"Because every single thing you say is usually stupid and ridiculous."

Teifert sighs. "Here's your assignment. And no, until we get our replacement slayer trained, you can't get out of this. We need you to go try out for the cheerleading squad. Infiltrate their ranks. Find out what's going on."

I stare at him aghast, too stunned to answer at first. Then I find my voice. "No effing way."

"Rayne, do I have to remind you of the nanos still in your blood?"

Ugh. Why does he always have to go there? Basically, for those of you just joining us, when they selected me as a potential slayer girl at birth, the nurse—a secret Slayer Inc. operative—injected me with some kind of nanovirus that lives in my bloodstream. And if I refuse a mission, all Slayer Inc. has to do is activate the virus and I'm dead. Nice, huh?

"But wait a second! I'm a vampire. I'm immortal. You can't threaten me with nanodeath anymore." Ha! Answer that one, T-Man!

"The nanos are encapsulated shards of wood. If activated, they'd head straight for your heart. Basically, you'd be staked from the inside out."

Um, wow. That's . . . wow.

I swallow hard before speaking. "It's not that I don't want to do this," I argue. Yeah, right. Do I sound convincing? "It's just that there's no way the cheerleaders are going to let me join their ranks. All teens may look alike to you, T, but take a closer look at yours truly. I'm not cheerleader material. I don't dress like a cheerleader, I don't talk like a cheerleader, I can't do splits or back handsprings to save my life. Oh, and there's the whole 'they are my archenemies and want to kick my ass' thing to contend with. There's no way in hell they're going to let me on the squad."

"Rayne, you're a smart girl. You'll figure out something," Teifert says. He gets up from his chair, reaches in his pocket, and hands me a hall pass. "Now you'd better get to first period. Don't want to get a detention the first day."

"But we're not finished talking. This is an impossible assignment. I mean, infiltrating seedy blood bars and staking evil vampires? That I can handle. Cheerleaders? No effing way."

"Good luck, Rayne," Teifert says, jumping off the stage and heading toward the main exit. "I'll expect a report from you in a week."

I slump into the folding chair, staring at my hall pass. Great. Just great.

3

"So then he says I have to join the cheerleading squad!"

My boyfriend, Jareth, reaches over to squeeze my hand in sympathy. His is squishy with suntan oil. A bit grossed out, I pull my hand away to wipe it on my towel.

Yes, it's after school and we're at the beach. Again. Sigh.

Ever since Jareth found out that the blood virus had bonded with the melanin in his skin and he was, for the first time in like a thousand years, able to go outside during the day, he's become the biggest sun worshipper to ever walk the earth. When we first met we'd go to dark, enchanting goth clubs and dance the night away. These days, all he wants to do is tan and surf. Yup. My perfect, pasty, eyeliner-wearing, Goth vampire boyfriend is now a beach bum.

I've tried to humor him. To be understanding. After all, I imagine it's been rough, sleeping in coffins for a millennium. And to finally get a chance to rejoin the human race? Yeah, that's got to be pretty enticing.

Still, I hate the beach.

"Well, look on the bright side. I bet you'll look pretty sexy in one of those short skirts," he teases.

I swat at him, careful to avoid his grease. Since he has no chance of developing skin cancer, he douses himself with baby oil every time. I, on the other hand, am fully clothed from head to toe and sitting under a black umbrella. The last thing I want to do is ruin my perfectly pale complexion.

"Whatever. I'm so not doing this. One, it'll ruin my rep. Imagine! Me! Rayne McDonald. A cheerleader! And two, they'd never, ever in a million years let me on the squad."

"That, I don't believe."

"What? Why not?"

"If you wanted to, you could get on that squad."

God, he can be so naïve. "No way. Look, Jareth," I argue, trying to be patient. "I know you were born a billion years ago, but let me tell you a little bit about twenty-first-century high school. There are two requirements to being a cheerleader: One, you have to be one of the Populars; and two, you have to be able to flip your legs over your head. Neither of which I have any chance of doing. Though I think the flipping thing would probably be easier, now that I think about it."

"You underestimate yourself, as always. Give away your power. Rayne . . ." Jareth turns to me, looking me straight in the eye. "What color is your parachute? And who moved your cheese?"

Ugh. Ever since he was forced to retire as General of the Blood Coven Army due to the blood disease's weakening effects, he's decided to learn new replacement skills so he can be known for his brains rather than his brawn. Problem is, instead of going back to school, taking night classes, whatever, he's decided to do this by stocking up on self-help books. And now every time we get into a discussion he starts quoting some sort of ridiculous psychobabble or other.

"Okay, okay. I'll try out for the squad," I relent. "I don't have much of a choice, anyway." Better to give in now, before I'm subjected to a lecture on how to win friends and influence cheerleaders. "Rah, rah, rah, and all that!"

"I just know you'll be brilliant, darling," Jareth murmurs, leaning over to kiss me softly. I close my eyes, enjoying the sensation of his lips on mine. He is an excellent kisser. And very sexy. And I love him to death . . . er, undeath, I guess. I mean, the guy literally sacrificed everything he had—his job, his vampire powers—all for me! How lucky am I to have a boyfriend like that?

It's just that—well, between you and me, and you'd better not say anything!—lately, he's been . . . different. More . . . cheerful, I guess you could say. Happy. Enjoying life. No more brooding. No more deep, dark secrets and heart-wrenching drama. Which is . . . good, right? I mean, it seems like it should be good. And it's not that I want him to live his life pent up, anguished, and miserable. Well, not exactly, anyway.

But you've got to understand, when I first met him he was so different. So much like me. The two of us were thrown together and quickly bonded through our mutual unhappiness with the hard, cold world. We came together as two lonely souls—desperate, tortured, filled with angst. We didn't trust. We didn't share. But there was a lot of dark, hot passion between us.

Now, ever since he's gotten me as a girlfriend and has been able to worship the sun again, he's been so . . . happy!

What's an Emo girl to do?

4

"Sunny, I need an extreme pep makeover."

My twin, sprawled on her stomach on her bed, looks up from her math homework, eyebrow raised. "Excuse me?" she asks. "I don't think I heard you right."

"I need you to turn me into a prep."

"Okay, now I know I didn't hear you right." She sits up. "What the heck are you talking about, Rayne?"

"Am I not speaking English here?" I ask, getting irritated. It's already embarrassing enough to be asking this to begin with. "I need you to turn me into a prep so that tomorrow afternoon I can try out for cheerleading."

Sunny bursts out laughing. She throws herself back on the bed, tears of mirth streaming down her cheeks as she hoots and cackles. I've obviously just said the funniest thing she's ever heard and it's going to take her a while to calm down.

"Um, whenever you're done . . ."

"Oh my God, Rayne," she says, shaking her head. "You're too funny. I just got this total image of you in a cheerleading uniform with fishnets and combat boots."

"Uh, yeah. Hence the makeover request."

"Wait, you're serious, aren't you? How can you be serious?"

"Come on, Sun. I asked you for a favor. Do we have to play Twenty Questions?"

"My sister, lover of the night, vampire of the Blood Coven, never before seen in anything but the color black, wants to be a pom-pom waving, football field–dancing cheerleader? And I'm not allowed to ask why?" Sunny snorts. "Yeah, right, Rayne. I'm not helping 'til you come clean. So what's the deal? You planning to play some crazy trick on them? Make them look like fools in front of the whole school? Come on, tell me. I promise not to squeal. I'm your twin, after all."

"Sunny, there's no plan. I've just got to make the squad."

Sunny stares at me, patiently.

"Okay, fine. I've been asked by Slayer Inc, to try out."

"Really? Are there evil vampires on the squad?"

"I don't . . . I don't think so," I say, "Though who knows? Mr. Teifert just said they thought something weird was going on. And he believes it has to do with Mike Stevens's disappearance."

"That's funny. I was thinking it was probably *you* who made Mike Stevens disappear. Met him in a dark alley one night this summer. Seduced him into your power, then BLAM! Bit him in the neck. Sucked every last drop of blood from that asshole's veins."

I cringe. "Uh, yeah. Right. Except I don't drink blood, re-member?"

"What? You're still on the synthetics?"

My face heats. How embarrassing. I've been a vampire all summer and I've yet to pick out a pair of Donor Boys and start living like one. The idea of drinking blood from another human being just grosses me out and I can't help it. I figured once I made the change I'd suddenly be ready to start sucking away. But no. Just the thought of digging my tiny fangs into someone's neck gives me the willies.

After nearly dying of starvation my first week, they put me on synthetic blood. Sort of like soy milk instead of cows' milk. It doesn't taste all that good, but it's better than down-ing the real stuff.

The coven doctors believe it may have to do with the fact I had the virus. I'm not quite human, but not full-blooded vampire. So while I can't stomach solid food without throwing up, I still crave it with a vengeance. And while I can't survive without human blood, I'm repulsed by the idea of drinking it.

I'm the coolest vampire ever. Not.

"Yes, I'm still on synthetics. So what?"

"Nothing. Just . . . it's weird."

"Not really. It's like . . . vegetarianism."

"A vegetarian vampire is weird."

"Wow. We've been here ten minutes and I'm not one bit prepped out yet."

"Fine, fine." Sunny groans, dragging herself off the bed. "Let's see what I can find." She walks over to her closet and starts rummaging through. "So Slayer Inc. thinks the cheerleaders have something to do with Mike's disappearance?"

"Yup. And he says they've been heard growling."

"Oh-kay then." Sunny laughs. "So you've got to secretly infiltrate their ranks and figure out where they stashed the quarterback."

"Something like that."

"What I want to know is how the heck you're going to make the squad."

"Extreme pep makeover, I told you."

"I hate to break it to you, Rayne, but it may not be that simple. One, they're going to see right through your pink clothes. Your tattoos won't be easy to cover up, just FYI. And two, regardless of whatever stereotype you have in your head, I gotta tell you, there are some minimum skill requirements for cheerleaders."

"Please. They just jump around and wave pom-poms. How hard can it be?"

Sunny shakes her head. "Fine. You'll see. But I suggest you practice before your tryout. A lot." She hands me a pair of yoga capris and a tank top. "Seriously. And even then, you're not going to be able to master a round-off back-handspring by tomorrow evening. There's going to be lots of girls more qualified than you."

"Yeah, yeah."

"Not to mention Mandy's the captain of the team. And we all know what Mandy thinks of you."

"Right," I say, suddenly inspired. Mandy Matterson. Captain of the squad. Former best friend. That gives me an idea.

"Sunny," I say. "Forget the makeover. I have a much better plan. One that will guarantee I make the squad, no questions asked."

Oh yeah, baby. This is going to be fun.

5

"Okay, we're going to call you out by name, one at a time. You'll step out in front of us and perform your cheer. Then we may ask you some questions. We only need two girls to fill the squad, so obviously most of you won't make it. We're very selective here at Oakridge High. We have standards. High standards."

After finishing her speech, Captain Mandy sits back down in her seat behind the row of tables, joining the seven senior squad members serving as judges today. She tosses her long blond hair behind her shoulders and clears her throat.

"Okay," she says, after a glance to her clipboard. "Up first, Britney Smith."

A giggling blond girl jumps up from the bench the rest of us wannabes are sitting on and cartwheels over to the center. Hmm, nice open.

"Hi!" she exclaims brightly. "I'm, like, Britney Smith. Thanks for having me!"

Do we get bonus points for over-the-top, air-headed behavior? Something to consider. Not that I think for one moment I'd be able to pull off that level of vapidness.

"I'm so nervous," squeaks a voice next to me. I turn to the girl in question. She's smaller than the rest of the hopefuls and really thin. The kind of girl who'd get to be top of the pyramid were she to make the squad. Still, she's not as . . . Barbie doll looking as the others. Her brown hair's a bit on the stringy side and her huge, unmade-up eyes are a muddy shade of brown. She's wearing a long-sleeved black shirt and baggy shorts that do nothing for her figure. I'd like to say those things don't matter and that it's all about talent, but I can't imagine that's a realistic assumption in this scenario.

"Meh, you'll be fine," I say, trying to calm her nerves. Not like I'm not a bundle of them myself.

"My mother was captain of the squad back in the 1970s when she went to Oakridge," the girl continues, her voice literally quaking with fear. "And she really wants me to follow in her footsteps. When I didn't make the team last year, she was so upset."

Wow. Talk about pressure. I hate parents like that. The ones who try to relive their own sad, pathetic youths by forcing their kids into activities they used to enjoy. Who knows, this mousy little girl could have been a terrific artist or track star. But she's going to waste all her effort in this air-headed, pseudosport because Mommy Dearest wants to be able to brag at bridge.

"Well, I'll keep my fingers crossed for you," I say. "I'm Rayne, by the way. What's your name?"

"I'm Caitlin. But everyone calls me Cait."

"Okay, Cait." I hold up my crossed fingers. "Good luck."

"Thanks, Rayne," she says, beaming back at me. She seems like a really nice kid. I hope that she gets picked. Me and her. That would be ideal.

"Up next, Cait Midwood." Mandy already sounds bored.

"Ooh!" Cait squeals, throwing herself at me for a hug. Did I mention I hate hugs? Or any kind of public displays of affection. After all, there's a three-foot bubble rule for a reason. But I endure it because I know she's so excited. "Here goes nothing! Wish me luck!"

"Luck!" I wish. And I mean it. Though I don't know how optimistic I am.

She bounces up from her seat and skips out into the center of the room. I watch as she starts in on a pretty elaborate cheer. Wow. Even I can tell that she's good. Really good. Almost as if her joints are made of springs, always bouncing from one trick or jump to the next. She ends the cheer with a round-off back-handspring, back-tuck, and then throws her arms up into a V, a huge smile on her face. She knows she's nailed it.

I'm so excited for her, I break out in applause, then realize no one else is clapping and lower my hands, a bit embarrassed. But whatever. She did an amazing job. Ten thousand times better than the girl before her. They'd be a fool not to accept her on the squad. Then again, they *are* fools, so really, all bets are off.

"Rayne McDonald."

Oh great. Here goes nothing.

I try to jump up from my seat as I saw the other girls do and bound across the gymnasium floor. Problem is, I manage to trip on my untied sneaker and fall flat on my face, slamming my knees against the shiny floor. Ugh. A rippling of laughter comes from the stupid peanut gallery.

I try to look as dignified as possible as I pick myself up off the floor and brush the dust off the tight, sexy yoga capris and tank Sunny let me borrow. (So not me, but at least they're black.) Then I head to my position.

"Hang on a second!" cries Mandy. "Rayne McDonald?"

Eight pairs of eyes stare at me from behind the tables, utter disbelief written on every Kewpie-doll face.

"Uh, yeah?" I ask, feigning complete innocence. "That's me!"

"Um, yes, we can see that. It's just . . . well, why are . . . *you* . . . trying out for cheerleading?" sputters the girl to Mandy's right.

I clear my throat. I've prepared for this very question. "Well, I just felt that lately Oakridge High has become a cesspool of dispirited youth and it would be irresponsible of me not to rise to the challenge of inspiriting our young people. To bring cheer to the uncheerable. Spirit to the spiritless. Joy to the unenjoyable."

Blank looks all around. Hmm.

I try again. "And I just, like, thought, like, it'd be really cool to be one of you guys?"

Ah, there are the head nods of understanding.

"I'm sorry," Mandy snorts. "But I really don't think you're cheerleader material."

"I see." I study her thoughtfully. "Yet, funny, I seem to re-call your flyer saying *everyone* is allowed to try out. I believe this rule is in response to some sort of Big Betty episode back in 2004?"

No one can say I didn't do my homework. A few years ago, the cheerleaders excluded some three-hundred-pound girl with facial acne from tryouts on the ruling that, well, she was fat and had zits. Turns out, according to the school's policy and procedures manual, that's not an acceptable reason to deny someone the opportunity to try out and her mother sued the school. Betty got enough money for plastic surgery and stomach stapling and last I heard she was living in Manhattan, modeling for Calvin Klein.

The cheerleaders murmur to themselves. Obviously it takes eight brains to come to one decision in this crowd. Good thing they have one another. I can't believe Mr. Teifert thinks these chicks are a threat to the school. I doubt they'd be a threat to a paper bag. I am so wasting my time here.

"Okay, fine," Mandy says at last. "You can try out. But don't get your hopes up. I hardly think you have much of a chance."

"Like, thanks!" I cry, all school spirit. I clap my hands. "You guys are the best!"

Mandy rolls her eyes. "Just go."

I jump into position, wishing I were a real vampire with powers. Preferably the power to flip and kick. Then this would be uber-easy.

Oh well. Here goes nothing.

"*Wolves, let's hear you yell go-GO*
 Wolves, let's hear you yell fight-FIGHT
 Wolves, let's hear you yell win-WIN

*Wolves, all together yell go fight win-*GO FIGHT WIN
GO FIGHT WIN!"

Ugh. I'm already out of breath and that's just the first
stanza. How do these girls last a whole football game doing
this crap? Forget part two. I'm ending this while the ending's
good.

I launch into a straddle jump—the kind where you're supposed to touch your toes with your hands. Unfortunately for
me, I'm sort of balance challenged and instead I end up fling-
ing myself backward and landing with a thud on the gymnasium floor.

"Goddamn it!" I cry, rubbing my bottom. If I wasn't a
vampire, I surely would have just broken my butt. Even as a
vampire I'm likely to end up with a nasty bruise.

"Um, thank you, Rayne, that was . . . interesting," Mandy
says. "We'll let you know."

I flash her a fake smile and then prance over to the bench.
Cait greets me and gives me a comforting squeeze. I can tell
she thinks I totally blew my chance.

"Are you coming?" she asks, hopping to her feet and gesturing to the locker room. "I think we're done."

"You go on," I tell her. "I'm going to watch the rest of the
girls."

"Okay," she says. "I hope you make the squad!"

"You, too," I say, smiling up at her, suddenly realizing I just may have the power to make her dreams come true as well. Power I plan to use.

Cait waves good-bye and walks away. I turn back to the tryouts. Some perfect blonde is doing some kind of bendy Cirque du Soleil–type movement. It hurts just to watch. Nice.

Anyway, after what seems an eternity, all the wannabes finish their tryouts. The cheerleaders dismiss them with haughty good-byes and insincere good lucks and begin exiting the gym. Mandy is the last to leave, gathering up all the score sheets and stuffing them in a manila envelope. Perfect.

I approach the table. "Hey, Mandy," I say casually.

She looks up, disdain and no friendly recognition on her face. I can't believe she and I were once BFFs. "I'm sorry, I can't tell you the results." She sniffs. "You'll have to wait until Monday like everyone else. Though I guess I could give you a hint. You ever hear the expression 'a cold day in hell?' "

"Actually, that's not it," I say sweetly, ignoring her jab. "I—well, I have this one other cheer I was working on. Sort of a custom-made, personalized thing. I was wondering if I could run it by you."

She frowns. "Look, you had your official audition, as per our rules. I'm not going to give you any bonus points for this."

"Oh, I don't want bonus points," I say, the picture of innocence. "I just want to see what you think of my cheer."

She sighs deeply, as if the weight of the world has just landed on her narrow, bony shoulders. "Fine, Rayne. Go ahead."

"Great!" I clap my hands. "You won't be sorry!"

I run to the center of the room and get into position.

"Ready! Go!" I cry.

> *"We've . . . got it made*
> *We're gonna win this race*
> *I have video of you with braces and a bad perm from*
> *seventh grade—*
> *That I'm gonna post on MySpace!"*

Okay, so the poetic stanzas don't exactly match up, but from the look on Mandy's face I think she gets my message.

> *"You've got a lot of baby fat*
> *You've got zits on your face*
> *Let me be a cheerleader . . . and, um, Cait, too. 'Cause*
> *she's all that!*
> *And the video I will erase!"*

"Rayne! Get the hell out of here!" Mandy hisses, her face pale and her eyes wide. Is the big, bad cheerleader actually trembling in fear? Ooh, you've got to love twenty-first-century blackmail. All you need is a camera phone and a laptop with wireless Internet to destroy their lives.

"Thanks, Mandy." I grin. "I really hope I make the squad. *Goooo*, Wolves!" I cry for good measure, before I skip off to the locker room, feeling pretty damn good about myself. I can feel her evil stare at my back the whole way.

Who knew becoming a cheerleader would be this much fun?

6

When I walk into school on Monday, the hallway is crowded with bouncy girls all scrambling to get a better glimpse at a certain piece of pink paper stuck up on the main office wall. Their desperation would make a less cynical girl imagine that the meaning of life itself is inscribed on that precious page. But I know better.

"Did I make it? Did I make it?" squeals one high-pitched voice amidst the mob.

Yep. Cheerleading picks.

I stand at the edge of the crowd, adopting a completely unconcerned expression as I patiently wait my turn. After all, I can't let anyone think I'm anxious to join the pod people. They'd never understand that, for me, making the squad is a matter of life or death, not some desperate stab at popularity. Well, technically it's a matter of undeath or death, seeing as I already abandoned the whole mortal coil thing when I became a vampire, but you know what I mean.

I squint, trying to make out the flowing, cursive handwriting from the back of the line. Did my plan work? Did my former friend Mandy sacrifice her standards to save her rep? Did the other lemmings go along with her recommendations without knowing why?

Did I, the worst cheerleading contestant in the entire country, actually make the Oakridge High squad?

Cait suddenly materializes in front of me, the tiny pixie having somehow managed to worm her way to the front of the mob and back again without suffering permanent bodily injury at the hands of the rah-rah wannabes.

Her eyes are bright and shiny and her face alive with excitement. "We made it!" she cries, bouncing up and down like she's on an invisible Pogo stick. "Oh, Rayne! We're cheerleaders!"

I smile and accept the hug she throws my way. She really loves the whole touchy-feely stuff. Still, her enthu-siasm and pure, unadulterated happiness warms me. I'm so glad I included her in my blackmail cheer. "Wow, that's great," I exclaim, feigning surprise and delight. "How lucky for us!"

"I know!" Cait says, releasing me from the hug. "I never thought I'd make it. I mean, I've been practicing forever. But my mom ..." She stops bouncing for a moment, a sheen of embarrassment coloring her cheeks. "Well, she wanted me to dye my hair and start sucking up to the popular kids. I tried to tell her that being a cheerleader requires athletic talent, not social standing, but she refused to believe me." The mousy girl pauses, a hurt look washing over her face. Then she shakes her head and flashes me a bright smile. "But this will show her! I did it all on my own. I made the squad 'cause I'm good, not because of who I'm friends with."

"That's great!" I say, guilt gnawing at my stomach. Am I no better than her mom? Discounting her because of her shabby clothes and hairstyle? Believing there was no way she'd make it unless I "helped?" Maybe if I'd just minded my own business . . .

I shake my head. It doesn't matter. Bottom line: She's made the squad and she deserves to be there, whether these morons needed help recognizing it or not. She's talented and enthusiastic and will be a great asset to the team.

Unlike, let's say, for example, me.

Because, I suddenly realize, making the squad is only step number one. Now I actually have to perform. Cheer and dance and not topple off the tops of pyramids.

This should be interesting.

So after school, instead of heading home to log in and edit my latest YouTube film or play video games with Spider, I instead trudge my way to the Oakridge High gymnasium. Ugh. I can't believe some people do this kind of thing willingly— stay at school longer than they're required to by Massachusetts law. I mean, sure, I suppose some of them just want to come off as "well-rounded" on their college apps, which I guess I understand. But evidently there's a certain contingency that joins clubs and teams and stuff because they actually think it's (shudder!) fun.

Once in the locker room, I change into the gym outfit Sunny loaned me. Black sports bra, blue tank top, and some dumb white shorts with SPIRIT written in big letters across the seat. I don't understand that fad at all. I mean, who in their right mind wants to willingly draw attention to their butt?

"Let's go, girls!" Mandy commands, clapping her hands together. She looks like a skinny bottle of Pepto-Bismol in her pink Juicy sweat suit, size zero. Her long blond hair has been swept up in a neat ponytail and her makeup is heavy been swept up in a neat ponytail and her makeup is heavy and flawless. "Time's a-wasting."

The other girls, in various states of undress, groan and hasten to slip on shorts and sneakers. I'm relieved to see most of them are just wearing normal raggedy gym clothes and aren't dolled up like our fearless leader. I'm not sure I could stomach being the sole ugly duckling in a chorus line of swans.

We head out into the gym and form two lines. I, unfortunately, am placed in the front row. So much for keeping a low profile. Mandy stands in front of us, like an aerobics instructor, and starts calling out the cheers.

I try to follow her movements without much luck. Damn it, I knew I should have watched that DVD they gave me to take home on Friday. You know, the one with the detailed cheering moves I was supposed to learn before the start of practice? I'd meant to watch it, of course, but then that night Spider had begged me to play video games with her for just "five minutes." Five hours later, when I finally logged off, it seemed too late to start bouncing up and down, waking the entire household with spirited yells of "Go Team!" And then Saturday was Get Your Blood On night at Club Fang. Like ladies' night, but for the undead—no cover for vamps! It seemed unwise to miss out on such a money-saving dancing opportunity. And then last night, well, last night I, um, was busy. Fine, okay, I just sat around and did nothing last night. In hindsight, I probably should have popped open the DVD instead of that pint of Ben & Jerry's Phish Food. (Especially since I threw it up a half hour later. Sometimes I hate being undead.)

I guess I just figured that it wouldn't be all that bad to just show up and wing it. After all, these mentally challenged Airhead Barbies could do it—how hard could it be?

Very hard, turns out. Very, very hard.

I listen to the commands, watch the others, and try to mimic their movements. But for some unknown reason, I keep getting it all wrong. They turn left, I invariably turn right. They jump forward as I'm jumping back. They clap down when I'm clapping up. I'm offbeat, uncoordinated, and clumsy.

For those of you who have never done it, I'll tell you right here and now: Cheerleading is *not* as easy as it looks.

Unless, of course, you're Cait. She looks like she was born with a megaphone in her hand. As if she's been on the squad her whole life. She's got all the right moves and is completely in sync with the others. So unfair.

"How do you know this stuff?" I hiss, after accidentally colliding with her.

She grins, obviously in her element. "My mom taught me a lot of it when I was a kid," she explains. "And I go to all the football games. I guess I've just kind of picked it up. Plus, you know, the DVD they gave us. I've probably watched it fifty times since Friday."

Oh. Yeah, that'll do it, I guess.

"Rayne, no! You're doing it all wrong!" Mandy screams, storming over to my spot in line. "Go left. No, no! Your other left. And put your hands up like this." She grabs my arm and yanks it above my head. "And your leg should be out like this." She kicks the inside of my calf to widen my stance. Problem is, the sudden movement knocks me completely off balance and I stumble forward, instinctively grabbing onto her to break my fall. A moment later we're both tumbling to the ground.

"Damn it, Rayne!"

I roll off of her, red-faced. "Sorry," I mutter.

This sucks. Totally sucks. I can't believe Teifert is making me do this. There has to be some Slayer Inc. rule banning the forced humiliation of its employees, no? If not, there should be. If ever there was cruel and unusual punishment, this would be it.

The other cheerleaders whisper amongst themselves, clearly annoyed that I'm wasting valuable practice time. I *told* Teifert this was a bad idea. I mean, sure, the blackmail worked like a charm to get me on the squad, but I'm never going to get them to like me enough to spill their growly little secrets in the locker room.

I pick myself up off the ground, trying to salvage what pride I have left. Nothing I can do about it now except try harder. Show them they were wrong about me. Hell, if

Airhead Barbies can do this cheering thing, so can Rayne McDonald. Right?

"Nancy, take Rayne over to the other end of the gym and show her some moves," Mandy orders, scrambling to her feet and brushing invisible dirt off her perfect sweat suit. She's probably furious that she's stuck with me for the season and pissed off she can't tell her squad why.

"What good's that going to do?" Nancy, the petite blonde in the back row, whines. "I mean, let's face it. She sucks. I don't get why you wanted her on the squad in the first place, Mandy. There were, like, fifteen other girls better than her."

Murmurs of agreement run through the squad. Mandy looks like she's been force-fed a cockroach. She opens her mouth to speak. Is she actually going to tell them what I did?

"Nancy, give her a break!" I whirl around, in shock. Holy crap. It's Shantel. Shantel's actually speaking up in my defense. "It's her first day."

"I don't give a damn if it's her first minute," Nancy says. "She sucks. Totally not cheerleader material."

"Obviously you don't remember *your* first day." Shantel sniffs. "You were on your butt so much we all thought you must own stock in BenGay."

I stifle a giggle. Go, Shantel! You tell her.

Nancy squeezes her well-manicured hands into fists, her face bright red, but doesn't reply. Probably trying to fire up her brain for a really good comeback. Which, I realize, could take a while.

"Look," Shantel continues, tossing her long black hair over her shoulder as she walks over to where I'm still sprawled out on the gym floor. "We're a team. And team-mates stick together." She offers her hand. I take it and she boosts me to my feet. "Come on, Rayne. Let's go to the other side of the gym and *I'll* work with you on the cheers."

"Whatever," Nancy growls. "Far be it for me to stop you from wasting your time."

Shantel ignores her and looks at me. "You ready?" she asks.

Shocked and grateful, I nod and then follow her down the court, away from the other cheerleaders. I can't believe she's being so nice to me. Does she have some ulterior motive? But no, what could she possibly have to gain by helping me?

"Thanks," I say when we're out of earshot. "That was really great."

"Don't mind Nancy," Shantel says, rolling her eyes. "She can be a real bitch. Gives us all a bad name." She shakes her head. "Most of the squad isn't like her though, I promise. And we all had to practice like crazy when we first joined. If you're willing to put in the work, I'm sure you'll be up to speed before our first game." She claps her hands together. "Ready?"

I am. And after about an hour of private practice, I start to catch on. Okay, I'm not ready to take part in an international competition or anything, but I haven't fallen on my face again. Shantel's a good teacher. Good at explaining things. Doesn't get annoyed when I mess up the same thing four times in a row. Uh, not that I did that. Really.

She's also a terrific athlete, I realize, as I watch her demonstrate a particularly impressive jump she calls a "Herkie." Great stamina, flexibility, and strength. She could probably play any sport and do well. I wonder why she chose cheerleading. Does she have some kind of deep insecurity that makes her want to wave pom-poms? If she does, she hides it well. On the surface she's, like, the most confident girl I've ever met.

"Thanks," I say when our session is over. "I think I'm getting it."

She grins. "No problem," she says. "See, it's pretty easy once you know what you're doing. And," she adds pointedly, "you practice."

"Yeah, yeah. I'll practice, don't worry." I laugh. "After all, I don't want to fall flat on my face come game time."

Shantel smiles. "It's all good. If you do, we'll pick you up again." She swings her arm around my shoulders and we head back to the main group. "You're one of us now, Rayne McDonald. An Oakridge High Wolf."

And for some strange reason, I'm suddenly okay with this.

7

The night of our first game is beautiful. The temperature perfect—mid-seventies—and the moon full and shining down on the field, almost bright enough to outshine the stadium lights. There's a crackling of electricity in the air as we exit the locker room and bound down to the sidelines of the Oakridge High football stadium dressed in our blue and white uniforms and carrying pom-poms.

We line up on the track, a blue gravel strip, in front of the home-side stands. I get into position, third from the left, and set my megaphone down on the pavement. It's then that I look up at the audience for the first time. There's got to be a million people up there. Or at least a hundred. Kids from school, parents, random townspeople. I had no idea so many people attended these things. I thought school spirit was only something you found in the movies.

What's worse is all these random citizens of Oakridge are all staring down at me. Watching me, probably judging me, waiting for me to fall flat on my face. Which, I fear, is very likely, judging from my track record.

I freeze in fear and almost drop my pom-poms. It's as if Medusa from *Clash of the Titans* is sitting in the stands and just struck me down, turning me into a stone rendition of my former self.

OMG, I can't do this.

I start to slowly creep out of position, hoping no one will notice my surreptitious exit. After all, I'm not really an essential part of this team, right? I'm only here on reconnaissance. They don't need me. Well, except for that one special pyramid, but they can forgo that one tonight, right? Find something else to do at halftime—

Shantel grabs me by the back of my sweater and yanks me back into position. "Where do you think you're going?" she hisses.

"Uh, I think I left my flatiron on," I mumble, my cheeks burning. "I have to go—"

"I don't care if your flatiron burns down the entire school. You're not leaving the field during a game."

"But . . ." I swallow hard, looking up at the humongous crowd and then back at her. My mind races, trying to come up with a good excuse, but I find myself too frazzled to be clever. "Argh! I can't do this!" I blurt out instead. The truth hurts.

She turns me around to face her, hands on my shoulders, her violet-colored eyes (contacts much?) staring into mine.

"You *can* do this. You've trained hard all week. You know the cheers. You know the pyramids. You're just suffering from stage fright."

"No, I'm not!" I retort, offended beyond belief. After all, I'm the Slayer. I vanquished an evil vampire and saved the world, for goodness sake. There's no way I'm afraid of some stupid humans at some stupid football game.

Am I?

"Those people?" Shantel continues, gesturing up at the throng in the stands. "All the girls want to be you. They want nothing more than to be standing on this very field wearing a cute skirt and sweater just like you. And the guys? They all want to be with you. They'd hook up with you in a second just so they could claim they dated a cheerleader. So no matter what you do, no matter how badly you screw up, they'll still worship you and want you." She grins. "Or if that doesn't help, you can always picture them in their underwear."

That I can do, in fact. For real. X-ray vision is one of the few vampire powers not gimped by the blood virus. I decide to give it a try, concentrating hard, finding the power within me. I let it rev up in my mind as Jareth taught me to do. Then I look back up at the people in the stands.

And start to laugh.

Mr. Gordon, our nerdy science teacher, is wearing boxer shorts depicting cupids and hearts. The French teacher, Mademoiselle Dubois, who all the boys are in love with? She's wearing very unsexy granny panties. And is that Miss Robinson, our more than pleasantly plump cafeteria lady, up on the last row, wearing a very tiny thong? Gross.

Shantel's right. I feel better already.

"Thanks," I say to her, after taking in a deep breath. "You're right. I feel better already."

Shantel gives me a thumbs-up. "No prob," she says. "First-nightitis. It happens to everyone."

The whistle blows and the game begins. They kick the ball. We kick our legs. They make a goal. We wave our pom-poms. It's kind of fun, in a weird way. And exciting, too. Especially when we're tied, 21/21 at the last few seconds of the fourth down (see, I've been studying!) and one of our players is set up to make the game-winning field goal.

"Go, team, go!" the cheerleaders cry, nearly breathless in their enthusiasm. They really do seem to care about the outcome of this game. Crazy. Though, at this moment, truth be told, I've got my fingers crossed for the home team as well.

"Too bad Mike Stevens isn't here," Cait whispers to me from my right. "Even though he's the quarterback, he's the best kicker."

I'm about to say Mike Stevens can go kick himself where it counts for all I care, but then I remember my mission. "Where is he these days?" I ask. "Haven't seen him around."

Mandy shoots me a sharp look. "He's nowhere. Don't worry about him," she scolds. "Just concentrate on the game."

Hmm, that seems a bit of a harsh answer to a very simple question. Maybe Teifert's right. Maybe the cheerleaders are holding some kind of secret. Or Mandy could just be a rude, no-mannered bitch. Actually, that seems more likely.

The players line up and number 17 gets ready to make the kick. I watch as he backs up, then runs forward, foot making contact with the ball and sending it soaring. The pigskin flies through the air. Everyone (including me) holds their breath.

It's . . . It's . . .

It's good!

The crowd goes wild. The cheerleaders bounce. I bounce, too, an electric excitement sparking through my body. I can't believe I'm this revved up over the outcome of a football game. After all, I'm not exactly the high school football type.

Maybe this skirt/sweater/pom-pom combo is slowly sucking brain cells from my head.

But whatever. We won. That's all that maters at the moment.

After the game we head to the locker room to change out of our uniforms. I've never been one to change in front of others, but the cheerleaders all whip off clothing like it's prom night. Soon, the room is filled with bra and lacy thong–clad girls, talking animatedly to one another. I guess if you have perfect bodies you don't need the modesty gene.

I notice across the room that Cait is the sole exception to the exhibitionism displayed in the locker room. She ducks into one of the bathroom stalls to change out of her uniform. And she emerges wearing a long-sleeved shirt and jeans. Which is somewhat weird, considering it's probably seventy degrees out.

I overhear whispers about an after party at Mandy's house to celebrate their victory, but no one invites me along. Not that I care. The last thing I want to do is go to some cheerleader party. Still, I can't help but feel a slight sting from being so obviously excluded. Stupid popular crowd.

I slip out of the locker room, ready to go home and back to my real life. Maybe I'll go see if Jareth's about. He's been acting kind of distant lately, and I'm hoping nothing is wrong. Maybe we'll go to Club Fang for a little dancing. Whatever. As long as I don't have to go home and face David, the now live-in boyfriend, and the toilet seat he forgot to put down. Being a Slayer Inc. operative, he'll want to know all about the cheerleaders and I really don't have any info on them except that they didn't want to talk about the missing Mike Stevens mid-game. Who knows, maybe they just didn't want to jinx the guy with the ball.

I've reached the gym exit. One push on the door and it's back to real life. But guilt gnaws at my insides and forces me to pause. A party is a perfect opportunity to learn more about the missing football player. To do recon for my Slayer mission. How can I just go home now? I've worked so hard to become one of them. To gain their trust. Now I've got to use it to my advantage. After all, up until this point I haven't learned anything. We've been practicing so hard there's been little time to socialize and find out the 411.

Tonight's the perfect night to do some recon. Even if it does mean attending a cheerleader party at my archenemy's house.

I reluctantly head back to the locker room entrance, wrap my hand around the door handle, and give it a pull. It doesn't budge. That's weird. Why would they lock the door? Are they happy to be rid of me and want to make sure I don't come back? Nah, that's stupid, right?

I rap on the door. "Hey! Let me in!" I cry. There's no answer. I put my ear to the door, trying to figure out what's going on. It's then that I hear a strange noise.

Almost like . . . growling.

I leap back from the door. Isn't that what Teifert had said to look out for? Girls that growl? But why would the Oakridge High squad be growling? It doesn't make any sense. I put my ear back to the door to get a better listen.

Growling, snapping, howling. Almost like there's a pack of rabid dogs behind the door. What the . . . ?

I yank on the door handle again, but it's stuck fast. What if they're in trouble? Cait's in there, after all! And Shantel! I bang on the door with both fists. "Let me in!" I cry. But there's no response. What if they're all being eaten by a pack of werewolves or something? Do werewolves even exist? I guess if vampires do, it's certainly possible . . .

Why, oh, why do I have to be a powerless vampire? My undead brothers and sisters would have no problem at all breaking down the door and rescuing those trapped inside. Me, I'd have to wait for a locksmith to show up before I could save the day. By then, everyone's likely to have been beaten to a bloody pulp.

Desperate, I send out a mental alert to any vamps in the vicinity. That's another one of the few powers I did inherit, go figure. Yup. I'm a supernatural creature of the night, whose superpower consists of . . . well, calling for help. And unfortunately I can only send, not receive answers. So I have no idea whether anyone's even paying attention.

A smashing of glass from behind the locked door brings me back from mental telepathy land. I hear a shuffling of feet and the growling fades into the distance. Whoever—*whatever*—it was making all that noise has evidently left the building. I've missed everything. I suck. Slayer Inc. is going to be so sorry they didn't get my replacement up to speed before doling out this latest gig.

"Rayne!" I whirl around and catch sight of Jareth striding across the gymnasium floor, an anxious look on his tanned face. "Are you all right?" he asks, approaching me and giving me a once-over with concerned eyes. "I heard your call for help and came as quickly as possible."

I sigh. "Great. Just what I need. Another powerless vamp," I mutter. I'd so been hoping Magnus or one of the other uninfected vamps heard my call for help. "Now we can both stand here looking stupid 'cause we can't break down a simple locked door."

Jareth's face falls and I instantly feel bad for opening my big mouth. After all, the guy used to be all-powerful. The impenetrable General of the Blood Coven Army. Until, of course, he willingly sacrificed all of his powers for the rest of eternity just to save my miserable little life.

How about a little gratitude, Rayne?

"Sorry," I mutter. "It's been a long night."

"Right," he answers stiffly. But he doesn't look completely appeased. Not that I blame him.

But now is not the time for apologies. "I need to get back into the locker room," I explain, gesturing to the door. "The cheerleaders are inside and there's been all this crazy growl- ing and glass breaking going on. I think they might be in danger!"

Jareth grabs the handle and pulls. To my shock, the door swings open with ease.

"What the hell?" I cry, staring at the door, amazed. "How did you do that? Did you get your powers back or some- thing?" Wow, wow, wow. If he got his powers back maybe I could, too. I'd become an all-powerful vamp just like every- one else.

Jareth shrugs. "It's just a door, Rayne. Even mere mortals can usually manage to pull them open once in a while."

I scrunch my face in confusion as I walk inside. "But just a moment ago it was—"

The words die in my throat as I get a good glimpse of the locker room. Or should I say what's left of it.

The place is trashed. The bathroom stall doors have been ripped from their hinges. Garbage cans have been turned on their sides, regurgitating used feminine hygiene products and other disgusting trash. Claw marks mar the shower stalls and the smoked glass windows at the far end of the room are smashed out.

But the cheerleaders are nowhere to be seen.

"And I thought guys' locker rooms were messy," Jareth remarks drily.

I approach the windows, trying to peer out into the night. Whoever caused this mess must have escaped through there. I notice something caught on one of the jagged glass shards and pull it free.

A tuft of hair. Like . . . dog hair.

I turn to Jareth, questioningly. "Jareth," I say softly, "are there such things as—?"

But Jareth, suddenly very alert, puts a finger to his mouth. I cock my head in question. What does he hear? He tiptoes over to the last bathroom stall, the only one left with a door on its hinges, and yanks it open.

"Don't hurt me!" cries a female voice inside.

I rush over. It's Cait. Curled up on the toilet seat so her feet don't show under the stall. Like she's hiding from some-one . . . or something. She's quivering, trembling.

And bleeding.

8

The smell of the blood dripping from a long cut on her left arm is nearly overwhelming. I imagine it sliding down my throat. Spicy, warm, and thick. So delicious. So satisfying. I take a step back. The girl's obviously been through something horrifying—the last thing she needs is some newbie vamp who's been denying herself proper food for the last few months to finally give in, grab her arm, and start sucking away.

I shake my head. I'll get a hamburger on the way home. Extra rare. No big deal. Really.

"Don't come any closer!" Cait cries, her hands in front of her face as if to ward off an impending blow.

"Cait! It's me. It's Rayne. Are you okay? You're obviously not okay."

I notice Jareth has taken a large step back as well. Probably fighting the same urge I am to suck. We vampires really turn into monsters when it comes to fresh blood. And resistance often is futile.

"Rayne?" Cait whimpers, lowering her hands and looking up at me. "Is that really you?"

"Hang on. I'm going to call 911, all right?" I rummage through my messenger bag for my cell phone, flip it open, and start to dial.

"No!" Cait protests, yanking her sweater down over her arm and jumping off the toilet seat. She grabs the phone out of my hand and volleys it across the room. It skitters over the tiled floor, battery popping off the back.

"Uh, was that really necessary?" I demand, now angry on top of bloodthirsty and concerned. That's the third phone I've gone through this year. And Mom's never going to buy that it wasn't me who broke it this time.

"You don't need to call 911. I'm fine."

"You're bleeding."

"Just a tiny cut. Not a big deal."

I scan the locker room, taking in the carnage. "Not a big deal? Look around, Cait. You're going to tell me nothing happened here?"

Cait's face crumbles and she bursts into tears. "No." She sobs. "Something did happen. Something really . . . crazy. I can't explain it. It's too . . . too weird. You're going to think I'm insane."

"I promise you, Cait. Absolutely nothing you say will make me think you're insane." I put a hand on her shoulder. "Seriously." If only she knew about me, she'd think I was the one who needed the men in white coats to take me away.

"I saw . . . with my own eyes . . ." She shakes her head and leans against the locker-room wall, staring up at the ceiling. I can't help but notice the blood from her cut is now soaking through her sleeve. I force my eyes away. "Oh God, you're going to think I'm nuts. But the cheerleaders. They . . . they . . . all of a sudden they—"

"Morphed into werewolves, trashed the place, and ran howling away into the night?" Jareth asks in a calm, matter-of-fact tone.

Cait's eyes grow wide as saucers as she stares at Jareth. "How did you know?" she demands, her voice trembling. "And who are you, anyway? And how did you get in the girls' locker room?"

"Don't worry, Cait. That's Jareth. My boyfriend. He's one of the good guys," I assure her. Then the enormity of what Jareth said hits me. I turn to him, my own eyes probably as wide as Cait's. "What did you just say?"

He shrugs, looking around the room. "From the evidence we see here, it seems quite possible that the entire squad has somehow been infected by the lycanthropy virus."

"Lycan—?"

"In layman's terms, they've been turned into werewolves."

"Ha, ha, ha, ha!" I fake laugh as hard and loud as I can, trying to pretend his statement is ridiculous and nothing we should seriously consider a problem. After all, I don't want Cait to think we're a couple of freaks who believe in things like that. The girl's been through enough already tonight. Last thing she needs is to be told that creatures of the night aren't just made up monsters in horror movies, but live and walk among us. "Jareth, darling, you're such a kidder! So silly. Werewolves. Ha, ha, ha!" My mind races for a more believable, less monster-driven theory as to why the cheerleaders trashed the gym and took off. Maybe it was their time of the month and they were really, really grumpy . . .

"Well, Rayne, actually it makes sense," Cait says slowly. "I mean, in an impossible way, but still. When I went into the bathroom to change, Mandy, Nancy, and the rest of the gang were their normal, beautiful selves. Blonde, blue-eyed, and certainly lacking any body hair whatsoever. Then when I came out, the locker room was filled with furry wolf women, running around like nutcases, howling up a storm, and destroying everything in their paths."

"Um. Yeah, but maybe someone . . ." I'm so reaching here. "Er, let a pack of . . . wild dogs in the locker room by mistake. You know, through a back door or something?"

Jareth shoots me a pointed look.

"What?" I ask. "It could happen! In fact, that's probably exactly what did happen. Pack of wild dogs. Maybe even coyotes. They left the door open and they just came in and—"

"The wolves were wearing bras and panties, Rayne."

"Oh."

Sigh. So much for convincing Cait the world is a normal, monster-free place. She's scarred for life. One of us now. I wonder if she'd like to apply to become a vampire. And if so, is there a signing bonus for bringing in new recruits?

Cait bursts into a fresh set of tears. "You guys think I'm crazy, don't you? Like one of those people always getting abducted by aliens. No one believes them either." She sniffles. "I know what I saw. They were werewolves. They were really werewolves."

"Rayne believes you," Jareth comforts, putting an arm around her shoulders. "She's just trying to protect you."

Cait buries her head in Jareth's chest, sobbing uncontrollably. He stiffens, probably at the proximity of the open wound beneath her sweater.

"What I want to know is how you got that cut on your arm. Did they . . . scratch you?" I ask cautiously. I don't want to freak the girl out even more than she is already, but we've got to be practical here. What if a simple scratch is all it takes to become infected by the werewolf bug? It's bad enough three quarters of the squad is currently out howling at the full moon and chomping on football players. I don't need Cait to start shapeshifting, too.

But Cait shakes her head, her cheeks blushing a tomato red. "No," she says. "I . . . that was just an old scratch that broke open when I ran to hide in the bathroom. It has nothing to do with the werewolves."

I narrow my eyes. She's lying. I know she is. But why? "Let me see it," I demand.

"No." She shakes her head vehemently.

"Come on, Cait. This is important." I try to grab her arm.

"I said, 'No!' " she cries, wrenching her arm free of my grasp and running toward the locker-room door. "I've got to go home! My mother's expecting me!"

"Wait—!"

The door slams behind her, echoing with a loud bang.

I start to run after her, but Jareth grabs my sweatshirt hood and reins me in. "Let her go," he says.

"But she's cut. What if she turns into a werewolf, too?" I protest. "And what if she goes around school telling everyone she's just witnessed Oakridge High's varsity cheerleaders morph into a pack of dogs? That would be really bad."

"First off, no one would believe her if she did," Jareth says calmly. "And second, I doubt she'd risk being the laughingstock of school by spouting what they'd think of as nonsense. More likely she's just going home."

"And the cut? Her mother will kill her if she turns into a werewolf next full moon."

"I'm not an expert, but I believe the lycanthropy virus is transmitted through saliva," Jareth explains. "So unless she was bitten or kissed by one of them, she's likely safe."

I think for a moment. "It definitely looked like a scratch more than a bite," I conclude. "So do you think that means she's going to be okay?"

"I think you'd be better off concerning yourself with the other girls," Jareth says, pacing the locker-room floor with long steps. "How did they catch the virus to begin with? As far as I know, there are no Lycan packs in the New England area. Slayer Inc., to their credit, has done a good job keeping the dogs out."

"You keep saying that. *Lycan*. What's 'lycan' mean?"

"Lycans are what humans refer to as werewolves. A human and wolf hybrid, which is usually a side effect of the lycanthropy virus. Similar to vampires, except that Lycans can live and walk as humans for much of the time. They only turn feral—into wolf form—when there's a full moon." Jareth glances out the broken locker-room window. "Like tonight."

"Gotcha," I say. "But why the hell would someone turn Oakridge High's cheerleading squad into a pack of wolves?"

"I have no idea," Jareth says, shrugging his shoulders. "But I would suggest you interview them tomorrow. Find out what they know."

"What should I say?" I ask. "I mean, I can't exactly be all, 'Hey girl, what big teeth you have!' " I giggle at the idea of using that line on Mandy. She'd be so pissed. "Or, like, 'So . . . you ever consider laser hair removal for all that fur?' Or I know! I could say, 'Wow, that nose job really gave you a snout and a half, huh? Are you suing your plastic surgeon?' And that's not even mentioning what I could say about tail."

Jareth smiles. "But seriously, Rayne. Be wary about confronting them straight out. They likely aren't aware of their actions when they morph into their feral state. In fact, they may assume they just blacked out from drinking too much and thus they don't remember what they did the night before."

"Makes sense," I say. "Though that makes it harder to get the real dirt on them."

"I'm sure you will manage."

"So then, when/if we find out what really happened to make them this way, how do we go about making it . . .

unhappen?" I ask. "I mean, is this forever, like a vampire? Or is the process somehow reversible?"

Jareth runs a hand through his hair. "I am not sure. I will have to do some research. I very much hope that we can find a cure. A pack of Lycans can cause tremendous problems when let loose in the suburbs."

"Problems?" I ask.

"They like to . . . snack," Jareth says wryly, and I'm pretty sure he doesn't mean on Strawberry Pop-Tarts.

"Oh my God! Do you think they ate Mike Stevens?" I ask, not sure whether to be horrified or secretly delighted. Then I scold myself. No one deserves to be eaten alive by a pack of Prada-clad puppies. Not even him. "Maybe that's why he's missing!"

"It's possible."

Bleh. Poor Mike Stevens. That's gotta be a terrible way to die. I think hard. "Okay, fine. I'll report this to Mr. Teifert in the morning and then go talk to the cheerleaders at lunchtime. Want to meet up after school to go over what I find out?"

"Sounds good. You'll find me at Hampton Beach. I've got a surf lesson at two." Jareth grins. "Hang tight, dude!"

Oh. My. God. He didn't just say, "Hang tight!" did he? Forget the lycanthropy virus. My boyfriend has been bitten by the Keanu Reeves bug.

"Um, sure. Hampton Beach. Whatever."

But as I leave the gym I realize I have more important problems than my boyfriend turning into a beach bum. The Oakridge High cheerleaders are werewolves. They may have killed the quarterback and infected my new friend.

And I, Rayne McDonald, am the only one who can stop them.

As usual. Sigh.

9

t's after ten when I finally get back to my house that night. Long past Mom's normal bedtime. But when I push open the front door I immediately notice three things at once:

- a light on in the kitchen;
- a delicious smell of food wafting through the air;
- the sound of my mom giggling.

I release a sigh. Great. David must have arrived. For some reason I'd been holding out hope that his move-in date was further into the school year and Mom was just giving us major advanced warning. But not so much, it seems.

I contemplate going in and saying good-night to the two of them, do the dutiful daughter thing and all. But then I reconsider. Seeing them together will only serve to make me sick. Mom turns into a total Stepford wife when she's around the guy and I can't stomach seeing her batting her eyelashes and saying things like, "Oh, you're so funny, David!" when he's clearly not even the least bit amusing. And then there's the authority figure act she tries to put on in front of him. She used to be Friend Mom—the one we could tell anything to and not worry about being judged. Now that she has David around to impress she's turned into Gestapo Mom—always ready to yell at me about one random thing or another. *Stop smoking. Start eating. Why don't you ever come home on time?* I can't remember the last time we had a long talk about life and stuff. Oh, and when I try to say anything about David she immediately gets totally defensive. I guess she never completely got over the time I told her he was an evil vampire. But that was an honest mistake and based on some pretty hard evidence. So not something she should hold against me.

I trudge up the steps and down the hall to my bedroom. I push open the door and switch on the light, glad to be back in my sanctuary. After the night I had I just want to decompress. Maybe play a few hours of World of Warcraft. It's Spider and my favorite online video game and we play every chance we get. In fact, maybe she's online right—

Oh. My. God.

At first I think I've stepped into the wrong room. This can't be my bedroom—my sacred escape from the brutal reality of the world we live in each day. *My* room has beautiful, dark, haunting photos on the wall. *My* room has a black comforter and is lit only by a single black-light bulb. *My* room has glow-in-the-dark stars on the walls and fake cobwebs strung from bedposts to ceiling.

The room I just entered is completely generic. The walls are bare, with only pinholes to show there'd ever been anything hanging on them. There are several new lamps, each with a gazillion-watt bulb, practically blinding me with brilliance. The bedding has been changed to a neutral navy blue spread and starched white sheets. There's even a few Glade PlugIns stuck surreptitiously into the plugs meant to charge my cell phone and iPod.

And there's a suitcase sitting on the end of the bed. With men's clothing spilling out of it.

"No, no, no, no!" I cry, horrified beyond belief. "This can't be happening!"

"I tried to stop her, Rayne, but she was a madwoman."

I turn around. Sunny's in the doorway, hair mussed and dressed for bed in flannel pajamas.

"Mom did this?" I cry.

Sunny puts a finger to her lips and motions for me to

Sunny puts a finger to her lips and motions for me to follow her into her room. I do, taking one last shuddering glance at the place formerly known as my bedroom. This time Mom has gone too far. Kicking me out of my own room! That's got to be breaking some kind of child protection law we have in this state, right? I wonder if DSS could step in here and stage an intervention if I tipped them off to her abusive parenting . . .

I should have never decided to keep living at home after I became a vampire. I should have moved out, gone to live in the coven with Jareth and the rest of my kind. That would have taught her to appreciate me. And I'm sure no one overdoses on Febreze in an underground crypt.

We step into Sunny's bedroom and she shuts the door behind us. I look around. Her room is completely untouched except for some kind of cot wedged in the corner. A cot! Mom expects me to toss and turn and likely suffer permanent back injuries in a rickety cot while her boyfriend snuggles down in a Sealy Posturepedic? That phone call to DSS is looking more and more like an option.

"I leave the house for one football game . . ." I mutter, not sure where to begin. I sink down onto the cot. It tips and groans under my weight. "I mean, at the very least she could have given my room away without the total makeover. Is David too good to sleep in a room with AFI posters on the wall? Is he allergic to fake spiderwebs and glow-in-the-dark stars?"

"It's 'cause you pissed her off by not cleaning it when she asked you to," Sunny explains, sitting cross-legged on her bed. Maybe if I'm really nice to her she'll let me sack out on her queen-sized tonight. After all, we're twins. We cuddled in the womb. Seems only fair now that one of us has been tossed out into the cold that the other start sharing. "When I came home after school she was up here looking at both of our rooms. Mine was pretty clean, like you see now. So I figured she'd just stick David in here."

That had been my thought as well. When Mom had told us we had three days to clean our bedrooms I realized it must be her clever ruse to pick the nicest one to stick her boyfriend in. And since Sunny's obviously too much of a Goody-Two–Shoes to disobey Mom (not to mention a total neat freak!) I figured I couldn't lose. Mom would take one look at my disaster of a bedroom and automatically pick my sister's room as the most David-friendly.

Guess Mom's more devious than she looks.

"This sucks!" I whine, lying back on the cot and staring up at the ceiling. "All my stuff. Where did she put it, anyway?"

"Basement, I think. She was muttering something about you getting it back when you learned not to be such a slob."

"Or when David the Dork decides to move back to Condo Land."

way those two get along, I'm wondering if he's here for the long haul. Mom's completely smitten."

I groan. "Sometimes I wish he really did turn out to be an evil vampire. Then we could have justified staking the guy."

"Oh, come on, Rayne. He's not that bad!" Sunny laughs. *Of course* she doesn't think so. She's still got her John Mayer–postered room intact.

"I mean, why can't she just shack up with the guy like a normal Mom? Have him share her bed? They're obviously sleeping together, right? I mean, they're adults. They've got to be. So why the separate room thing?"

Sunny shrugs. "Probably wants to set a good example for us."

"Bleh. Thanks, Mom." I sigh, shifting positions on the cot. "You know, Sun, you should totally go hook up with Magnus. Screw his brains out. Just to prove the point that her pathetic attempt at a morality lesson is completely ineffectual."

"Yeah, right. I'm not going to lose my virginity just to teach Mom a lesson, Rayne."

"Well, it's not like you wouldn't get anything out of the deal yourself," I grumble, annoyed that Sunny can't see the logic of taking one for the team. I'd do it myself, but I'm pretty sure Mom already knows I've been to home plate a few times by now.

"Anyway," Sunny says. "You'll never guess who I bumped into last night." She looks at me expectantly.

"Er, if I'll never guess, then why don't you just tell me?"

She pauses for dramatic effect. "Race Jameson."

I roll my eyes. Race Jameson is this rock star that everyone and their mother is obsessed with these days. He sings for a band called Triage and has become totally overexposed. I used to think his music was halfway decent until the band started appearing on TRL and stuff. Sellouts. Even the cheerleaders are obsessed with the guy these days. And let's just say it's not his music that's got their attention.

"Is he as good-looking in person as he is on MTV?"

Sunny grins. "Better. Much better. And . . ." Another dramatic pause. "He's a vampire."

I raise an eyebrow. *Now* she's surprised me.

"A vampire? Are you sure about that?"

"Yup. I met him when I was down at the coven last night, visiting Magnus. He's in the area for a month while he records his new album. I guess he'd been undead for nearly a thousand years, living on the down low until one day he picked up an Anne Rice book and decided Lestat shouldn't be the only vampire to rock 'n' roll."

"Huh. That's kind of cool," I admit, suddenly having newfound respect for the guy. Even if his music does suck.

"So anyway, how did the game go? Your first night as a cheerleader?" Sunny queries. "I still can't picture you in the skirt."

I roll my eyes. "Don't give me that crap. You know you went and watched."

Sunny feigns shock. "You think I went to the game? Risked your threat of slow death and dismemberment like the victims in the *Saw* movies if I came within a hundred yards of the field?"

"Duh."

"Okay, fine," my twin confesses. "I went by. Just for a few minutes to check out your moves. Actually, Rayne, you weren't half-bad. I was pretty surprised."

"Um, thanks. I think." I prop myself up on my side with my elbow. "Glad to hear you had such confidence in me. What did you expect? For me to fall flat on my face?"

"Rayne, face it, you're not exactly cheerleader material. Piercings and pom-poms don't usually mix."

"I'm not saying it's my scene. But my assignment was to become a cheerleader and I take my assignments seriously."

Sunny raises an eyebrow. "Uh, since when?"

"Anyway," I say. "I have bigger problems than mastering the megaphone at the moment."

"Oh?" Sunny crawls to the foot of the bed, her eyes dancing with mischief. "Like what? You fell for a football player? Developed a longing for lip gloss? You're now suddenly passionate about pink?"

I throw a pillow at her. "I'm serious!" I cry. "You do remember *why* I joined the squad, don't you? And, FYI, it wasn't for invites to the cool kids' keggers."

"I know, I know. I'm just teasing." Sunny laughs. "Slayer Inc. forced you to infiltrate the ranks of your archenemies to determine if they've been growling."

"Right." I nod. "And turns out they've been growling, all right. Growling, snarling, snapping. Not to mention sprouting hair. And claws. And teeth."

Sunny stares at me. "What the hell are you talking about, Rayne?"

"Sunny, Oakridge High cheerleading squad? They're actually a pack of werewolves."

"What? I—I mean . . . Do they even exist? That's crazy!"

"Is it? I mean, we know vampires exist. So why not werewolves? Hell, at this point I wouldn't even rule out the Easter Bunny and the Tooth Fairy."

Sunny shakes her head in disbelief. "But at Oakridge? I mean, Mandy Matterson and Shantel Jones and the rest? They're werewolves?"

"It appears so." I relate the events of the night to her. She listens, silent and wide-eyed.

"So what are you going to do?" she asks when I'm done.

I shrug. "I'm not sure. This is beyond my expertise, really. It's not like I can stake the entire squad. Besides, I don't even think that would work. Isn't it, like, silver bullets with werewolves? Something along those lines? And I don't know about you, but my concealed weapon permit has long expired. Plus there's that whole waiting-period thing—"

Sunny rolls her eyes. "In any case, you don't want to shoot the squad either, right? I mean, who would rally the crowd when we're down 21–3?"

I laugh. "Right. Plus it's one of those things that tends to get a lot of media attention. Not to mention prison time. And imagine if they gave me life in prison as a vampire? Eternity's an awful long time to stay behind bars."

"So what are you going to do then? Is there a cure or something?"

"I don't know. Jareth's going to look into it. And I'm going to have a little chat with the cheerleaders tomorrow—assuming they're back to their nonhairy selves. Maybe they can shed—ha ha, get it? Shed—some light on where and when they got bitten." I shrug. "Maybe if we know that we can figure out a way to reverse the process."

"Hopefully the cure doesn't involve the Holy Grail again," Sunny says. "That was a total pain in the ass to get our hands on. And expensive, too. Mag paid a million pounds to those druids. I doubt Slayer Inc. has that kind of budget."

"Still, we have to do whatever it takes to stop them," I say. "Who knows what trouble they'll get into out on the streets? I just hope they don't hurt anyone."

"Do you really think they did something to Mike? Like . . . ate him or something?"

I make a face. "I really hope not. But I intend to find out."

"At least you got a while, right? When's the next full moon?"

I grab a calendar off Sunny's wall. It has pictures of silly-looking dogs in costume. Figures. I flip to October. "According to this . . . it's October 15th."

Sunny's eyes widen. "Really?"

"Why? What's so significant about that date?" I ask.

"Rayne, that's homecoming."

10

I walk into the cafeteria the next morning and notice Shantel sitting alone at a far table. While seeing someone sitting alone in the caf might not normally set off any warning bells, for Shantel, it's a five-alarm fire. When not at cheering practice, the girl is always with her boyfriend, Trevor. And I mean *always*. The two of them are constantly locking lips or performing some other disgusting PDA that no one wants to watch before A period.

But today, she's alone and looking pretty distraught, too. Her always perfectly flat-ironed hair is tangled and unbrushed. Her makeup is smeared. And worst of all, she's wearing stripes with plaid. Something's very wrong here.

I approach her cautiously. "What's wrong, Shantel?" I ask, trying to keep my voice light. "You look like someone just killed your best friend." As soon as the joke's left my mouth I realize it's not all that funny. In fact, it could be exactly her problem.

She looks up at me with mascara-stained eyes. "It's Trevor." She sniffs. "He's missing."

My heart sinks. Another football team member has disappeared? On the very night the girls turned into werewolves? This is not good. Not good at all.

"Are you sure?" I press, sitting down beside her. "Maybe he just slept in. Or he has a hangover from that party you guys went to last night." I cross my fingers under the table, praying for a logical explanation, even though it's obvious there's not going to be one in this case.

Shantel shakes her head. "No," she says. "His mom called me this morning. Said he never came home last night. She was hoping he was with me."

Little did Trevor's mom know that was the last place she wanted her son.

"Did you see him after the game?" I ask.

"I went up to him on the field for a minute to congratulate him before we headed back to the locker rooms to change for the party. That was the last time I saw him." Shantel pauses, staring off into space. "And that's the weirdest thing, Rayne. I don't even remember the party. After the locker room, it's, like, a total blank. I don't know if I drank too much or someone slipped something in my drink. But I woke up the next morning naked in my bed. And I was filthy dirty—my hands, my knees, my feet. As if I'd been running around on all fours or something. Really, really weird."

So Jareth was right. She didn't remember a thing about her metamorphosis. Which was probably for the best, now that I think about it. Especially if it turns out Shantel and the others chowed on her boyfriend as a post-game snack. That kind of thing would definitely scar a person for life.

"Don't worry, Shantel," I say, patting her on the arm, trying to sound unconcerned and comforting. "He probably just got wasted and passed out somewhere. I'm sure he'll call you any minute now."

"But what about Mike Stevens?" Shantel counters. "He's been missing a month now. What if whatever psycho killer killed him went after Trevor, too? What if the guy's like a modern-day Jack the Ripper, but instead of going after prostitutes, he goes after football players? Maybe 'cause, like, he didn't make the team long ago and is now seeking revenge?"

It's not a bad scenario for a made-for-TV horror movie and certainly would seem a lot more plausible to your average person than the possibility of the two guys being eaten by rabid, cheerleading wolves. But I don't think it's healthy for Shantel to focus on either scenario at the moment.

"You're jumping to crazy conclusions," I scold. "And we don't even know that Mike Stevens is dead either. It's not like anyone's found a body. Maybe he just got sick of Massachusetts and took off to Europe or something. You know, to, like, go find himself." I'm totally stretching here, but hopefully she's willing to grasp at any straws at this point.

"You know, I'd like to go back to Europe myself at this point," Shantel blubbers, breaking into a fresh round of tears. "Everything's sucked so badly this year. I just want it to be over."

"Have you been to Europe? What countries did you visit?" I ask, trying to steer her into more comforting territory. Maybe I can get her off the subject and calm her down.

"We went to Europe for our cheerleading competition this summer," Shantel says, sniffing, wiping her eyes with her sleeve. "It was in the middle-of-nowhere England and we stayed at the cutest little village. The local people were so sweet. Though so superstitious. They were always warning us not to go out at night. Which, of course, sucked." She rolls her eyes. "But the last night we all decided to sneak out once everyone had gone to bed. We met up with this really hot English soccer player. You should have seen him, Rayne. He must have spent, like, years in the gym to get a build like that fine body of his. I swear, he looked exactly like a blond Brad Pitt. We were all totally in love. Anyway, he brought us to an amazing bonfire party in the middle of the woods. We all got so totally wasted. I don't think any of us remembered how we got back to the hotel. It was killer."

I stare at her. Tiny village in England? Night out in the woods that they don't remember? Could that be where they got infected? It has to be!

"Shantel, I've got to go," I say, rising from my seat. "But hang in there. I'm sure Trevor will turn up sooner or later. You'll see."

"Thanks, Rayne," she says, staring down at her hands. "I hope so. I really hope so."

Me, too.

"And so then Shantel says that they went to England for a cheering competition and ended up partying in the woods and they all blacked out. It's got to be where they were infected, don't you think?"

Mr. Teifert shifts on his throne. The drama class is doing *Camelot* this semester and so the auditorium stage has been transformed into a medieval kingdom. He thinks for a moment, then nods slowly.

"That seems like a logical explanation," he says. "But werewolves!" He shudders. "Can't have those running around town. We'll have to put them to sleep as soon as possible." He rises to his feet. "Thank you, Rayne. Job well done. We can take over from here."

What? Did he just say—?

"We can't put them to sleep!" I cry, jumping up to my feet. "That's like cruelty to . . . pep squads!"

"We'll use humane euthanasia, of course," Teifert says, not seeming the least concerned at the idea of the impending cheerleader genocide.

"But don't you think someone would notice if the entire cheerleading squad turned up dead?" I demand.

"We'd make it look like an accident," Teifert says with a shrug. "A bus crash, maybe a drunk-driving incident after a party. I mean, it's not like Veronica Mars is going to show up and start asking questions." He snorts at his oh-so-clever, yet completely outdated pop-culture reference, then turns serious. "Look, Rayne, these girls are monsters and can cause serious problems for our community. Look at what they did last night!" He passes me a newspaper. The front-page headline is "Vandals!" and the accompanying photo illustrates the word very effectively. The wolves evidently wreaked havoc on the entire town, breaking into department stores and destroying makeup counters, tearing through the local chocolate factory, and devouring all their goods. Ditto to three convenience stores—cleaning them clear out of Ho Hos and Ding Dongs. Hopefully, all this ravaging burned a lot of calories or these girls will *so* have to go on Atkins to fit into their size-two uniforms.

"Wow," I murmer. "I had no idea they did all this."

"Not to mention that they don't even have their shots," Teifert adds. "You want them running around town infecting more and more people? Pretty soon our town will be one big werewolf pack."

"But still!" I put the paper down. "They're not just were-wolves! They're teenage girls! And no matter how ditzy they are, they don't deserve to die."

"Look, Rayne, Slayer Inc.'s job is to police our community's supernatural element. To slay when necessary those who step out of line. These are not vampires living in secluded communities, keeping to themselves and not interfering with human life. They're a pack of wild dogs running around destroying everything in their path. I don't think you fully understand the danger here. They could break into your house. Kill your mother. Or worse, turn her into a werewolf. And then what would you do? Imagine finding out your mom's now a real bitch 'cause you were soft on fur."

"I know," I say, slumping into my chair. "I mean, I understand what you're saying. We can't let them continually ravage the town every full moon. But at the same time, there's got to be another alternative to just killing them."

"Like what?"

"Like . . . an antidote. I mean, that town in England. The one the cheerleaders stayed at after their competition. If that's where the biting occurred, maybe the townspeople know some way to reverse the curse."

Teifert is silent for a moment, then he nods. "Very well, Rayne," he says. "If you'd like to go to England and find out if there is a cure, Slayer Inc. will support the move. After all, we have a month before the next transformation. But if you can't find anything on your travels, then we will be forced to proceed with our plan."

"Great!" I exclaim. "Thank you so much. You won't be sorry. I'll find the cure. We'll get them back to their old fur-free selves."

"I hope so, Rayne," Teifert says, wearily. "Because I'm not sure our town can take another night like last night."

Right. Once again it's all up to me, Rayne McDonald, to save the world.

How do I get myself into these things?

After school, I head to the beach. I find Jareth there, wearing brightly colored Bermuda shorts and lying on a Corona beach towel. Oh, how cool. Not. I still can't believe my beautiful creature of the night has suddenly become tackier than a bottle of Super Glue. But how do I tell him he's lost all sense of style and dignity? Especially when he looks so radiantly happy?

"Rayne!" he cries, scrambling up to greet me. I jump back to avoid being hugged by a six-foot sand monster. I mean, I'm happy to see him, but have you ever had sand in your underwear? It's so not worth the affection.

"Hey, Jareth," I say, opening my black umbrella and holding it over my head to avoid any late-afternoon rays. Some of us vampires still have standards.

He looks hurt at the hug rejection and I immediately feel bad. This is my boyfriend, the love of my life. So why am I feeling so icky around him lately? Why can't I just be happy that he's happy? Why does he suddenly annoy me so much?

And the worse thing is, we're stuck together! Forever. This isn't like a regular BF/GF kind of thing where we can break up and never speak to one another again. Jareth gave up everything to be with me—to become my blood mate. And we are supposed to be together forever with no chance of a divorce! Scary. So very scary.

But whatever. I can't think of this now. Not when Oakridge High cheerleaders are chomping on football players. Relationship stuff can be figured out at a later date.

"So," I say, seating myself daintily on a beach chair, careful to avoid as much sand as possible. "I think I know where the cheerleaders became infected."

"Oh?" Jareth asks, plopping down on his towel, back to business as well. At least he's not so sunstroked that he can't concentrate on the task at hand. After all, he was once the guy who led a vampire army. "Where is that?"

I tell him what Shantel told me, about the cheering competition in England, the small spooky village, and the bonfire in the woods they don't remember leaving.

He nods thoughtfully, grabbing handfuls of sand and streaming them through his long fingers. He does have very elegant hands. Though they're tanned now, instead of their former beautiful, pasty white.

"It makes sense," he says at last, "that there is some kind of pack over there. But why would they infect American cheerleaders?"

"Well, why not?"

"True Lycan packs are very much like vampires and live under the same kinds of rules. The packs have to remain small and unobtrusive. In fact, I believe usually the only way to become a Lycan is to be born one."

"So then why . . . ?" That's so weird. Why would a pack of Lycans want to infect a squad of cheerleaders, only to send them on their merry way?

Jareth shrugs. "I don't know. But we need to find out. And fast."

"Can we go to England? Check out the village and see what we can learn?" I remember how jealous I was when Sunny went to England last year to find the Holy Grail and turn herself back into a human. I can't help but be excited that now it's my turn.

Jareth strokes his chin. "Yes, I think that's a good idea. We'll stay the first night in our sister coven. You'll get to meet some of the English vampires this way. And they should know where we can find the pack. I'll charter the coven plane for tomorrow night."

"Tomorrow night?" I scrunch up my face. "But we have practice—" I stop, realizing how dumb I sound. I've only been a pseudocheerleader on assignment. Now that I've figured out the mystery, there's no reason to keep showing up in uniform.

Still, that said, the girls are depending on me. Cait's depending on me. And Shantel. Until they can get someone else, I'm an essential part of the pyramid.

"Jareth, let's go on Friday night instead," I propose. "I've got . . . things to do. And after all, we have until the next full moon to figure this out. There's plenty of time."

Jareth shrugs and agrees, luckily not asking why. 'Cause how embarrassing would it be to tell him the truth?

That I can't go on saving the world if it means neglecting my duties as a cheerleader.

11

The next day after school we have cheerleading practice. And let me tell you, it's more than a bit weird to chill with girls who you know have a habit of turning into wolves, devouring football players, and going house on your hometown each full moon. But since I know they can't remember all their extracurricular activities, I have to remind myself that in all actuality, I'm pretty darn safe.

Poor Shantel's practically comatose over her lost BF and can barely concentrate on her moves. I really, really hope it doesn't turn out that she ate the guy. That's the kind of thing that could really mess up a girl.

Cait looks even worse. She's shaking like a leaf and keeping her distance from the other girls. Not that I blame her. Seeing your teammates transform into a pack of dogs doesn't exactly help create a circle of trust. Still, doesn't she get that we have to play it cool? We don't want the cheerleaders suspicious. They keep asking her what's wrong and she can only stammer nonsensical answers in reply.

"Okay, Cait," Mandy says, clapping her hands. "We're going to practice the Hitch pyramid. So come on over and we'll boost you up."

Cait stares at her, eyes wide. I can tell that the last thing she wants is any of them to touch her. I wish I could pull her aside for a moment. Reassure her that the girls have no idea she saw what she saw. Tell her she's perfectly safe, at least until the next full moon. And by then I will have figured out a way to stop the madness. (I'm so confident, huh?)

"Go on, Cait," I urge her. She glances over at me, her face white as a ghost, and shakes her head vehemently.

"I—I can't do it!" she whispers to me. "I just keep thinking that they'll—"

"Come on, Cait! We don't bite!" teases Shantel.

Cait shoots me one more pleading, terrified look and then sprints straight to the locker room. The other cheerleaders groan and jump down from their pyramid.

"What the hell's wrong with her?" Mandy demands, glaring at me accusingly. She's evidently still pissed that I blackmailed her into having Cait join the squad in the first place. Even though she has to have realized by now that Cait is way good—a great asset and hands down the best gymnast on the team. When she's not scared for her life, that is. I mean, gotta give the girl a break in this case. But Mandy, of course, has no idea. "We've got a game next week and we've got a lot of work to do to prepare for it. These cheers don't shout themselves, you know. And we can't afford to have girls on the squad who don't take being a Wolf seriously."

The Wolf pack—er, squad, all nod in sync.

"Why did we pick her, anyway?" demands one of the girls.

"Yeah, she's not even cute."

"Oh please, she's the best girl on the team and you all know it," I interject. "And she's been perfectly dedicated since she joined. So she's having a bad day. Give the girl a break."

I get a few reluctant grumbles of agreement. Good.

"Well, I'll go talk to her," Mandy says. "See what's wrong."

"Let me," I say quickly. The last thing Cait needs is to be trapped in a locker room with someone she thinks will sprout fangs and claws at any given moment. "I'll calm her down."

"Fine. But get back fast. We've got a lot of ground to cover this afternoon."

I nod and walk briskly toward the locker-room door, ready to comfort poor Cait. She must be freaking out. I remember how hard Sunny took the whole "vampires are real and I'm going to become one in a week" shock that first night at Club Fang. It's amazing how some people can live their whole lives perfectly oblivious to what's beneath the surface reality of our world. But once you've discovered the truth, there's no turning back.

I push open the locker-room door and once again am suddenly overwhelmed by the smell of fresh blood. I double over, hands on my knees, trying to catch my breath and control my almost unstoppable urge to run to its source and dig in. The thirst consumes me: My throat's suddenly dry as a church group dance and my nostrils strain toward the smell. Jareth warned me about this. The longer I go without drinking real blood, the more power it will have over me. But this is the worst yet.

I manage to suck a few shallow breaths through my mouth, as they taught us to do in Blood 101 class, and swallow hard before righting myself.

I'm okay. I can control the bloodlust. It has no real power over me.

I stumble to my locker where I keep a secret stash of synthetic. I fumble with the combination, rip open the door, and grab the sports bottle. I gulp the fake blood down, rejoicing as the thick red liquid coats my throat and settles my stomach. Ah, much better.

A moment later my head's clearer. Only then can I focus on the fact that smelling blood in a high school locker room could be something I need to be concerned with. I mean, sure, it might just be someone's time of the month, but for some reason I don't think it's that simple in this case. Where is the blood coming from? And, more important, where's Cait?

"Cait!" I cry, eyes darting from one end of the room to the other. "Are you okay?"

There's no answer. Just the drip, drip, drip of a leaky shower. Other than that, complete silence.

Fear grips my heart. What if one of the werewolves didn't turn back to a cheerleader when daylight hit? What if it's after Cait? What if it's already found her and managed to rip her apart? Could the blood that I smell actually be coming from Cait's mutilated, dead body?

Panicked, I start whipping back shower curtains, running through rows of lockers, and pulling open bathroom stall doors. She has to be in here somewhere. The only exit—through the window broken by the wolves last night—has been boarded up.

I reach the handicap stall and yank the door open.

Oh. My. God.

I stare down, eyes bulging with shock and horror. Cait's sitting on the toilet, fully dressed, with her forearm out in front of her. And it's covered in tiny bloody cuts.

At first I think somehow this is related to the werewolves, but then I notice the razor blade she's trying to hide behind her back.

"What are you doing?" I cry. "Are you trying to kill yourself? I'm calling 911!"

"No!" she says, jumping up, blood droplets splattering everywhere, some landing on my own cheering sweater as she grabs my arm. Argh. I feel like I'm going to pass out from the irresistibleness of the sight and smell of fresh blood—getting the nearly overwhelming urge to just latch onto her wound with my little fangs and start sucking away.

Sometimes being a vampire is really sick.

"Rayne, stop!" Cait begs, her eyes as wide and frightened as I'm sure mine are. "I'm not trying to kill myself! I swear."

I stare at her, suspiciously, while my insides war for blood-drinking dominance. "Cait, you're sitting in the bathroom holding a razor. You're bleeding. What else would you be doing?"

She turns deep red, leaning back against the wall and sinking down to a seated position. I scramble down on my knees and grab her arm for a better look. It's then that I notice the scars. There have to be hundreds of them. Crisscrossing up and down her arm—tiny silver threads, permanent reminders of past cuts from days gone by. Either she's attempted and failed suicide many, many times before or . . .

"You're a cutter!" I whisper, horrified and fascinated all at the same time.

I've read about girls like her. Those who get comfort from self-mutilation. When they get stressed or upset or scared or helpless they reach for a razor. The physical pain is supposed to soothe them emotionally. A lot of Goths and Emos do it for attention—for some pathetic reason they think it's cool—but real cutters simply can't help themselves.

Cait bursts into tears and wrenches her arm away from my grasp, pulling down her sleeve to cover the cuts and scars. "Please don't tell anyone!" she cries, tears streaming down her cheeks, smudging her makeup. "It's so embarrassing."

"Embarrassing?" I stare at her. "Cait, it's dangerous! You could seriously hurt yourself. Even if you don't mean to. You need to stop."

"I . . . I can't stop." Her blush deepens and she stares down at her lap. "I've . . . I've tried. I just can't."

Wow. This is more serious than I thought. Poor Cait. Suffering in secret for God knows how long. I grab her and pull her into a hug, trying to ignore the blood that's pulsating from her arm and radiating desire to all the pleasure sensors in my brain.

"Drink!" the vampire in me begs. But I ignore it. I have to.

"You *can* stop. But maybe you need help. We can get you some. Maybe your mother could get you an appointment with—"

"No!" Cait says, pulling away from the hug, her eyes wide as saucers. "Not my mother. She'd kill me!"

"If you don't get help, you're going to end up killing yourself."

Cait hangs her head. "I know," she says. "But please don't tell my mother. She was so happy when I made the cheerleading squad. For the first time in my life she's actually proud of me. I don't want to disappoint her again."

I squeeze my hands into fists, frustrated beyond belief. How stupid some parents are! Forcing their children to live the lives they want them to lead, even if those lives are far from what the children actually want for themselves. And for what? So the parents can look good when bragging about their offspring at cocktail parties? So they can relive their own glory days through their children? All her life Cait's been belittled by her mom. For not being cool enough, not being pretty enough, not being good enough to become a cheerleader like she was. No wonder the girl's mutilating herself. She has to release the pressure somehow.

"Cait, if your mom loves you she's going to understand you need help," I say, crossing my fingers that this is true. "Cutting is a sickness. Like diabetes or cancer. You can't help it. And you can't cure it on your own. You need help. Surely she will get that and find you some. And if she's disappointed in you—well, that's her problem. Not yours. You're awesome. You rock. Anyone who doesn't see that is a blind-ass moron who should be shot."

Cait giggles a bit through her tears. "Maybe you're right," she says. "I don't know. I just— Well, I just don't want to let my mom down, you know? Since my dad died, I'm all she has in the world."

"Maybe you could start by going to a school counselor or something. I think they have to be confidential, right? Unless you tell them you want to kill yourself, which I don't think is what's going on here. In any case, they could at least point you in the right direction and maybe help you figure out the best way to eventually break the news to your mom."

Cait opens her mouth to speak, but at that moment the locker-room door bangs open. Great. Just what I need. An interruption right before Cait promises she'll go get help.

"Rayne?"

Ah, even better. An interruption from my dear friend Mandy.

"I'll get rid of her," I say to Cait. "Get back in the bathroom so she doesn't see you."

Cait obeys, closing the stall door behind her. I breathe a sigh of relief. The last thing Mandy needs to see is Cait in this state—crying and bleeding. She'd probably use it as an excuse to kick her off the squad.

Mandy turns the corner and I jump in front of the stall door. She frowns. "What are you doing?" she demands, hands on her hips.

I gaze at her with wide, innocent eyes. "Nothing, Mandy," I say. "Nothing at all."

"You'd better not be doing drugs, freak. You signed a pledge, remember? Cheerleaders just say no."

I roll my eyes. "Just because I dress in black and listen to the Cure doesn't mean I'm some smackhead, you know."

"Yeah, well . . ." Mandy seems to be searching for a clever comeback, but none materializes. "What about Cait? What was with that freak-out? I don't want girls on my squad who can't handle the pressure. If she can't take the heat, she needs to get out of the frying pan."

"Nice mixed metaphor, Mand. And don't worry about Cait. She can take the heat. She's just having a bad day. You remember bad days, right? Before you became popular you had a lot of them, as I recall." I know I shouldn't be taunting her, riling her up even further, but I can't help it. She's such a self-centered bitch. Thinking the world revolves around her and her cheerleaders. Scorning anyone who isn't exactly like herself. I can't believe the two of us used to be friends.

"Whatever, Rayne," Mandy says, again with the awesome comeback. She really should join an improv group, she's so quick on her feet. "And you'd better be right. After all, if it wasn't for you, she wouldn't be on the squad to begin with."

I cringe. She had to go there.

Please don't let Cait hear what she said. Please don't let Cait hear what she said—

A small cry of surprise and indignation sounds from behind the stall door.

Great. She heard.

Mandy stares at me and her gaze drifts to the door I'm blocking. "What are you hiding, Rayne?" she demands, raising a perfectly arched eyebrow.

"Cait is talented, Mandy," I argue, ignoring her question. "In fact, I'd bet my belly-button ring that she's the most talented girl on the squad. You can go and say anything about me. I know I'm not Wolf material. But you know as well as anyone that she's amazing and deserves to be on the squad."

"The only thing that ugly little troll deserves is to be back on the math team where she belongs," Mandy returns, looking smug. I realize she knows exactly who I'm hiding and she's really mean enough to go there. "And if you didn't *blackmail* me into putting her on the squad in the first place, she'd be there right now."

I'm thrown forward as the bathroom door slams into my back. Cait pushes past me, running straight for the exit. I catch a glimpse of her tear-stained face and horrified eyes before she exits the locker room.

I turn to Mandy. She's totally the cat who ate the canary with her self-satisfied smile. I hope she chokes on the feathers.

"Why would you say that? You knew she was in there! How can you be so cruel?" I demand, hands on my hips. "When did you become such an uber-bitch, Mandy?"

"When did you become such an *uber*-softie?" Mandy fires back.

"What the hell are you talking about?"

"Oh please. Don't get all high and mighty on me, Rayne McDonald. You're first in line when it comes to judging someone based on their fashion sense."

"Me? Yeah, right. I've never turned down a friend because she doesn't carry this year's Prada purse."

"No? Well, how about one who mistakenly wears jeans to a Goth club and embarrasses you in front of all your new friends? Or one who actually—shock, horror—admits she likes high school football and has the nerve to ask if you'd lower your coolness standards for one night to go to a game with her? Or how about a friend who makes the cheerleading squad? Do you congratulate her on her accomplishment and say you can't wait to see her perform? Or do you have the nerve to ask her if the judging was based on hair highlighting and lip gloss selection alone?"

I open my mouth to respond, but suddenly nothing comes out. Did I really do and say all those things to her? Is that why she hates me so much?

"You always say the cheerleaders are elitist snobs," Mandy continues. "But as far as I see it, you Goths are just as bad, if not worse."

Before I can say anything she turns and stomps out of the locker room. The door slams behind her with an echoing bang.

My stomach twists into knots and I feel like I'm going to throw up. Is that really what everyone thinks of me? Am I just as bad as the cheerleaders? Condemning anyone who I deem less cool than me? Of course, maybe Mandy's just projecting—to make herself feel better. But still . . .

I shake my head. No time to dwell on my own possible shortcomings. I've got to find Cait before she does something else to hurt herself.

I push open the locker-room door and head out into the gym. The cheerleaders are sitting on the bleachers chatting amongst themselves. Mandy's nowhere to be seen.

"Have you seen Cait?" I ask.

Shantel gestures toward the exit. "Ran out," she says. "She looked really upset, too. What's up with her? Is she okay?"

"Mandy," I say, as if that could explain everything. "I've got to go find her. I'll catch you guys later."

I run outside, following the paved path that leads from the gym to the football field. I find Cait down by the bleachers, crouched on the ground, head in her hands, sobbing.

"Cait? Are you okay?" I ask, approaching her cautiously.

"Go away!" she cries, waving a dismissive hand in my general direction. "You've done enough."

"Cait, don't let Mandy get to you. She's a bitch and everyone knows it." I lean down to put a comforting hand on her shoulder. She swats it away.

"What did she mean, Rayne?"

I swallow hard, my mind racing for believable lies. But nothing's coming to mind. "About what?" I ask, stalling for time.

Cait looks up at me, an angry, accusatory look on her tear-stained face. "What did she mean when she said you blackmailed her to put me on the squad?"

"Um, I don't know," I say, laughing nervously. "Who knows what that girl means half the time! She's so dumb she—"

Cait scrambles to her feet, hands on hips, looking furious. I take a step back, worried she might actually try to hit me. "Don't lie to me, Rayne!" she cries. "I can't take any more lies." She squeezes her small hands into fists. Her whole body is shaking with fury. "Tell me the truth. Did you or did you not have something to do with me getting on the squad?"

I stare down at the ground. Time to come clean, I guess. Just hope she'll understand I only had the best intentions . . .

"Um, well, sort of," I stammer. "But only 'cause I thought you were so good. That you were better than anyone trying out. And I didn't want them to discount you because . . . because . . ."

I trail off. What can I say? Because you don't have highlighted hair? Because your clothes are frumpy? Because I didn't think your athletic skill would overcome your lack of style?

"Because I'm not cool enough to be a cheerleader," Cait finishes. "Of course. And you figured you'd help." She shakes her head, looking defeated. "God, how could I have been so stupid? To think they took me 'cause I was good enough. My mom was right. I'm not cut out to be a cheerleader."

"But you are!" I protest. "You're, like, the most talented cheerleader on the squad!"

"How would you know?" Cait asks, narrowing her eyes. "You suck."

Ouch. I wince. That hurt. Sure, I'm not the most natural cheerleader in the world. But I have been practicing. In fact, I thought I was getting pretty good—

"What I don't get is why you're even on the squad to begin with, Rayne. You don't like it. And you obviously think you're so superior to the rest of the girls. Why are you wasting your time? Filling up a slot that could be taken by some girl who actually enjoys waving pom-poms."

"Uh, well, actually that's a long story . . ."

Cait rolls her eyes. "Whatever, Rayne. Just eff off and leave me alone."

She storms off. I watch her go, wishing I could stop her, to tell her that she's totally off base. But I guess in all actuality, she's not. After all, I *am* only on the squad to infiltrate the werewolf pack. To accomplish my mission, not have a good time, learn skills, and meet new friends. But weirdly enough, I also kind of enjoy it now. It's kind of fun in an odd way. And I do like a lot of the other girls . . .

(Please do *not* tell anyone, ever, that I just admitted that or I will hunt you down and kill you slowly with much torture!)

I slump to the ground, furious at myself and the situation. Why did I think interfering with Cait's life was a good idea? I mean, I know I had the best intentions. But still! Now she'll never know if she would have made the squad on her own merit or if the only reason she's here is because of my stupid blackmail trick.

Mandy's right. I'm no better than the rest of them.

12

Too depressed to go back to cheerleading practice, I decide to head home. When I walk in the front door I'm greeted by the most glorious smell in the entire universe. Like a bug to a light I'm drawn to the kitchen, practically salivating over the aroma.

I find David at the stove, wearing my mom's apron, and stirring something in a pot. Ugh. For some crazy reason I was holding out some inane hope that my mom had somehow taken cooking lessons and was responsible for the delicious food currently being prepared. Even though I knew that was about as likely as Paris Hilton getting her MBA and launching her own accounting firm.

I consider turning around and fleeing, running to my room—er, Sunny's room—but realize it's too late to do so in a way that wouldn't make David think I'm purposely avoiding him. Even though, of course, I am. But I suppose I've got to face him at some point and it might as well be when I'm in as bad a mood as I am now. After all, the night can't get any worse at this point.

"Good evening, Rayne," he says, turning to me, a big smile on his face. "How was school?"

Oh nice. I love how in the short time he's been here he's made himself so at home in *our* house. As if he belongs here and pays half the mortgage. Not to mention how he seems to think it's his job to play Daddy since poor Sunny and I are essentially without that whole father-figure thing. Next thing you know he's going to start asking how my grades are shaping up and if I need help on my homework.

"Fine," I mutter, opening the fridge to rummage through longingly. I'm so hungry. Well, not hungry exactly, but craving food. Chocolate, ice cream, baked potatoes—heck I'd even take some of my mother's hippie hash or tofu burgers at this point. Just something to chomp down on, savor, and swallow.

I had thought that once I became a vampire all I'd crave was blood. I had no idea how much I'd miss chocolate chip cookies, pasta, and pizza. I'd almost sacrifice immortality at this point, just for one more Krispy Kreme donut.

"What are you cooking?" I ask, against my better judgment. I don't want to engage in any sort of meaningful conversation with the intruder—make him feel like he's welcome or something—but my mouth is watering and my curiosity overcomes my good sense.

"Vegetable soup," he says, walking over to the counter and picking up a knife. I watch, enthralled, as he dices a carrot. He grabs the slices and throws them in the pot. "I figured since this is a house filled with vegetarians, I'd better start learning to just say no to my meat-and-potatoes lifestyle and learn some new recipes."

I breathe in through my nose, savoring the soup smell. So good. So, so good. I have to fight the urge not to push him out of the way, grab the pot, and dump the whole thing down my throat in one gulp.

"Well, it smells delish," I admit.

"Sorry you won't be able to have any," he says in an overly sympathetic tone. "It must be hard to give up food." David works for Slayer Inc. and is one of the few people on earth that knows I'm now a vamp. All I can say is he better never tell my mom.

I scowl. "What makes you think I want any?"

"The drool at the corner of your lips," he says with a chuckle.

Oh. I reach up to wipe my mouth with my sleeve.

"That's not from soup envy," I explain, even though of course it is. "It's the bloodlust. I'm actually contemplating sinking my teeth into your jugular and sucking all the blood out of you until you're completely dry and shriveled up." I don't know why, but I find it amusing to try to shock and anger him.

Unfortunately for me, he doesn't take the bait. "Sure you are," he says with a patronizing smile. "You forget I have access to your file, my dear. I know you're still on synthetics."

"You looked at my file?" I cry, up until this moment not even aware I had a file. But if I do, I know I sure as hell don't want my mom's boyfriend checking it out! "What right do you have to look in my file?"

"I'm your guardian," he says simply. "It's my job to know these things."

"Well, I'm going to tell Slayer Inc. I want a new guardian. Or no guardian at all. You're my mom's boyfriend. There's gotta be a conflict of interest in there somewhere."

"I checked out the rules and I assure you, Rayne, it's perfectly on the up and up," David says. "And speaking of, how is your latest assignment going? Teifert tells me the cheerleaders are actually Lycans?"

I open my mouth to retort that it's none of his business when my mom walks in. All talks of the fanged and furry must cease.

"Hi, honey," Mom says, coming over to kiss me on the forehead. "How was school?"

I want to tell her about the football game. About my stupid English teacher who believes he's the greatest author since Shakespeare and forces us to sit and endure his poetry during class. And about a whole slew of other things that daughters share with their moms. But *he's* here. And I don't want him knowing anything about my life that he doesn't have to. He already knows too much—having looked into my file and all.

"Fine," I say, going the one-word answer route.

It doesn't matter anyway. Mom's already moved on to David, evidently feeling the one standard question satisfies her obligatory daughter-discussion requirement for the night. She walks up behind him and wraps her arms around his waist. He turns around, soup spoon in hand. She opens her mouth and he gives her a taste.

"Mmm," she says. "Delicious." She stands on her tiptoes to kiss him on the mouth. So gross. I turn away. "You're a great cook, sweetie. Much better than I could ever be."

"The neighbor's dog is a better cook than you'll ever be, Mom," I mutter.

Mom's face falls and I feel bad for being snarky. She tries hard. And she's never had any help. And look at her—she's happy! With a great guy who cooks. Why can't I be okay with that? But I can't be. I'm just too annoyed.

"Your mother is a fine cook," David scolds me. "And she works very hard. You guys should appreciate all she does for you."

Now he's lecturing me about being nice to my mom. I can't stand it! I'm always nice to my mom. Okay, well, the neighbor's dog jab wasn't exactly a Mother Teresa moment, but really, I'm a good daughter with lots of respect for the Momster. He so needs to mind his own business.

"Mom knows I appreciate her," I snarl. "And you're not my father."

"No," David says under his breath so Mom can't hear. "If I were your father I'd be off in the high-stakes poker room in Vegas."

That's it. I'm not going to take this from him. Not father cracks. Not when he should know how sensitive a subject that is with me. (If he'd read my file and all!) I start to lunge toward him, ready to attack. "You take that back!" I cry, shoving him in the chest. I catch him off balance and he falls back against the stove, making it look like my push was a lot harder than it really was.

"Rayne!" my mom cries, horrified and furious. She jumps between the two of us before I can take another swing at him. "Stop it! Now! What's wrong with you?"

David stares at me with cool eyes, as if daring me to keep going. I curl my hands into fists and take a deep breath, reminding myself that in addition to being my mom's boyfriend he also works for Slayer Inc. How much power does he have over there, anyway? Could he tell Teifert about my outburst and get me nanoed?

I look at my mom. She's sunk into a kitchen chair, head in her hands. Is she crying? God, that stupid David made her cry. He so deserves me to kick his ass.

"You bastard!" I say, furious. "Look at what you've done! You made my mother cry."

"I didn't," David says calmly. "*You* did."

I look at my mom, waiting for her to defend me. To speak up and say that David should leave and that she'd made a big mistake asking him to live here. That she's very sorry she put me and Sunny through all this and wants us to be a girls-only family again.

But Mom doesn't say any of this. And when David walks over to her and puts an arm around her shoulders she leans into him, sobbing against his chest. I stare at them, realizing I've been replaced.

"Fine," I say, giving up. "I see how it is. I'm so out of here."

I walk up to my room (sorry, make that *Sunny's* room) and start stuffing my clothes into garbage bags. First I'll go to England and then when I get back I'm going straight to the coven and moving in there. Or I'll hitch a ride to Vegas and shack up with Dad. Whatever. Just as long as I don't have to come home to Casa Unwelcome Rayne anymore.

You know, I hope Mom worries. I hope she thinks I'm dead and calls the National Guard or whoever you call when someone disappears. It will serve her right for siding with *him* instead of her own daughter. Her own flesh and blood. Bitch.

I can't believe how much everything sucks. I thought becoming a vampire would make all my problems go away.

So how come now I seem to have more problems than ever?

13

"I'm ready to go to England," I tell Jareth, cradling the cell phone between my head and neck as I peel out of the driveway in my Volkswagen Bug a few minutes later. I've so got to get one of those earpieces before I suffer permanent neck injury. "Let's go tonight. I'm on my way over to the coven now. I'll be there in ten minutes."

There's silence on the end of the line. "I thought you didn't want to go until Friday," Jareth says at last. "Don't you have school tomorrow? What are you going to tell your mother?"

"Screw school," I retort, anger burning in my belly. "I have eternity to get my diploma. No big deal if I flunk this semester. And Mom's easy. I'll just have Spider say I'm staying at her house. Worst comes to worst, Sunny can play both of us. She owes me. I mean, whatever it takes, right? The cheerleaders need their antidote. Though honestly I think at least one of them would be better off put to sleep. Think we can selectively apply it?"

A car honks as I cut in front of it at the last minute. I give the driver the finger. No one messes with Rayne McDonald, mad vamp gone postal, tonight.

"What's that honking? Are you talking while driving again?"

"Uh, no. I'm, uh, well, maybe. I'm fine though. Not a problem."

"You sound angry," Jareth says. "Did something happen?"

"No! Well, yes, but it wasn't my fault! I mean, all I was trying to do was protect her . . ." I trail off as the lump in my throat makes it nearly impossible to speak. I swerve to miss a black cat crossing the street. Nice. Some bad luck to go along with my bad day.

"Rayne, you don't sound fit to drive. Pull over and I'll come get you."

Oh great. Now he's going to start in on me. This is the last thing I need. I'm so sick of everyone trying to play Raynie's Dad. (Besides my actual biological father, of course.) I'm not helpless. I'm not in need of discipline. I can take care of myself.

Everyone just needs to eff off and leave me alone. Trust me that I can make good decisions and take care of myself.

I slam on the brakes to avoid colliding with the car in front of me, which for some ridiculous reason decided to stop in front of a yellow light.

"Learn to drive!" I yell out my window, my face burning with rage. I've half a mind to get out of the car and go bang on his window, fangs bared. Scare the life out of him.

"Rayne, pull the car over. Now!" Jareth yells into my ear, interrupting my horror-movie fantasy. Grr.

"No! I told you I'm fine. Stop being so damn overprotective," I growl back. "I'm a vampire. Your blood mate. Not some child. Stop treating me like one."

A pause on the other end of the line. "I didn't mean to imply . . ."

The light turns green and we start going again. I swerve to the left to try to pass the yellow-light stopper, but then realize there's a truck in the other lane. I swerve back, growling to myself. In response to my aggression, the other car suddenly slows down, forcing me to slam on my brakes again. My tires squeal against the pavement.

"What was that noise?" Jareth demands. "Rayne! Pull over the car. Now! You're scaring me."

"I'm *fine!* God, it's bad enough I have one random guy in my house trying to masquerade as my father. I don't need you to play long-lost Daddy, too."

"I'm not trying to father you. I just don't want you an angry splatter on the side of the road. Is that so much to ask?"

"I'm a vampire! I'm not going to splatter," I remind him. "I'm hanging up now. I'll be there in ten. Pack your bags for England." I click the End button and toss the phone onto the seat. A second later it starts ringing again. I reach for the radio and turn it up full blast, allowing Morrissey's crooning to drown out the ringtone.

When I look up from the radio, I see the other car for the first time, coming out of nowhere, headlights blinding me. I have a split second to realize I must have swerved into the wrong lane while turning on the radio. I spin the wheel. Unfortunately, I end up spinning it right into a guardrail.

The car slams into the barrier. I'm thrown forward. The air bag goes off with a poof, slamming into my face. A moment later I swim into blackness.

"Rayne, Rayne! Wake up!"

"Mmmm," I moan. "Five more minutes, Mom."

"It's Jareth, not your mom. And you've been in a car accident."

I open my eyes, suddenly remembering my close encounter of the guardrail kind. I'm sitting in the driver's seat still, an inflated air bag pushing into my chest. Jareth is outside the car, peering in with a concerned expression on his face.

"Don't say I told you so," I mutter as I crawl out of the vehicle. I take a look at my car. The hood's crumpled and there's smoke coming out of the engine. Great. Mom's going to kill me. So's Sunny, considering we share this car.

"Rayne, are you crazy?" Jareth demands. "Did you hit your head too hard? Why would I say I told you so? I'm just glad you're okay!"

I roll my eyes. "I'm a vampire, remember? I can't die. And look, my injuries are already half healed." I gesture to the bloody cuts on my arm, sealing up before my eyes. Way cool. I should try skydiving next. Or some other extreme sport.

"I know, but . . ." Jareth stares at me, looking helpless and upset. Part of me wants to go over and hug him, but the other part, the angry, bitter, hates-the-world part, doesn't want to give him the satisfaction.

"I'm fine. What I'd like to do is go to England now."

"But you've just been in an accident. We need to get you to a doctor or something."

"I'm fine!" I repeat. "Stop smothering me!"

Jareth takes a step back, as if he's been slapped. He stares at me, then shakes his head. "You know, Rayne," he says, "sometimes when people first become vampires they don't adjust smoothly. It takes some time and counseling to get used to their new existences. We have a great coven doctor who specializes at making transformations smoother—"

"You want me to go to see a shrink?" I cry.

"Well, we don't really call them that in the vampire world, but—"

"You do. You think I'm crazy!"

"No. I think you're angry. Angry enough to put yourself in a situation where you could get seriously hurt."

"For the last time, I'm a vampire! I can't *get* hurt. Can you get that through your thick skull? And secondly, for your information, I have plenty of reasons to be mad."

"I'm sure you do," Jareth says, reaching over to stroke my cheek. "But that doesn't mean you want to live your life like this."

I whack his hand away. "Maybe I do, okay? What are you going to do about it?"

The anger inside of me is building to frightening propor-tions. I just want to lash out and hurt someone, but there's no one who deserves my wrath. So I slam my fist into my car. Then kick it with my boot. I may not have vampire strength, but I still manage a few satisfying dents. I keep kicking, chan-neling all my hatred into my Volkswagen Bug.

"This is for you, Mandy! You self-centered bitch!" I bel-low as I kick. "And this is for you, Mom! How dare you side with David over me! And David! You're not my dad, you bastard! And this is for—"

"Rayne! Stop it! Just stop it now!" Jareth cries. "Destroying your car is not going to help things!"

What does he know? It's helping a lot. And he should be grateful I'm not kicking his ass instead.

He grabs me. I kick and scream, but he's too strong for me to escape. He may not have his vampire superstrength, but he's still a guy. I struggle to free myself for a few minutes, then reluctantly give up, suddenly weary of the whole ordeal.

I just want to go home. To my own bed. But I have no home or bed. I'm an undead creature of the night. Destined to roam the earth alone.

"Come on," Jareth says, loosening his hold. "Let's go back to the coven."

The next morning I wake up in a beautifully carved four-poster bed. The room is richly decorated, with fancy jewel-toned paintings and a fire roaring in a mammoth stone fireplace. My head still feels thick and foggy, but at the same time I feel very relaxed. Almost drugged.

"Are you feeling better?"

The voice makes me turn my head. I realize Jareth's sitting at my bedside, reading some self-help book. He sets it down on the coffee table. "You had quite a fit out there, Rayne."

"Yeah, sorry," I mumble. Wow. In the comfort of this cozy room I'm feeling pretty dumb and immature about what I did. "I don't know what came over me. I was just so mad."

"I noticed," Jareth says wryly. "You have some issues you need to work out, my dear."

I sigh. "I know. I'm sorry. You must think I'm the biggest loser."

"Not at all." Jareth crawls into bed next to me and strokes my head. "You're just going through a tough time. It's natural for a new vamp to have some adjustment issues. You've got new hormones raging through your body. It'll take a while for them all to settle. It's a bit like hitting puberty and it affects different vampires in different ways."

Great. So what do I have, PMS? Pre-Monster Syndrome?

"Well, I promise to be better behaved from now on," I say. "Really."

"I still think you need to see a counselor. We have a great one in the coven. He'll help you deal with some of your anger issues. Give you methods to control your rage."

Yeah, right. I'm so not seeing a shrink. "Uh, maybe. Sure. We'll see when I get back from England."

Jareth pauses, mid-stroke. "Um, about that," he says. "I think it might be better if I go myself."

"What?"

"You're in no shape to travel. I want you to stay here in the coven until you've seen the doctor and he's prescribed you some medication."

"No way! I can't take a mental holiday while the cheerleaders are running around eating people!" I protest.

"I think you need it," Jareth determines. "But don't worry. I'll go to England and get the antidote myself."

I struggle to sit up in bed. My cuts are all healed, but my head still hurts. "But it's my job. My duty. My destiny. After all, I'm the slayer."

"Rayne, you don't always have to be so tough. Relax. Let someone who loves you do something for you for once."

"No. I'm going and that's all there is to it."

Jareth frowns. "I'm sorry, Rayne, but that's not going to happen."

"You can't stop me."

"Actually, I can. I've set a guard outside this door."

"What?" I cry. I run over to the door and try to yank it open. It doesn't budge. "You've kidnapped me?"

Jareth rolls his eyes. "Oh, Rayne, stop being so overdramatic. This is for your own protection."

"But I need to go to England!"

"You don't. I said I'd go and I will. In fact, I'll leave tonight, just as scheduled. I'll get the antidote and bring it back."

"But what if you can't?"

"Thanks for the vote of confidence."

"But . . ." I realize my protests are useless. The bastard isn't going to give in. I wander back over to the bed and slump into my pillows. I'm trapped here, helpless, while he goes and saves the day. Just because I happened to run into a guardrail. I'm not sick. I don't need help. I just had a car accident. I shouldn't be under house arrest for it.

Jareth's such a jerk. And he treats me like I'm a child. I bet Magnus never treats Sunny like that. In fact, I bet Sunny gets to do whatever—

A lightbulb goes off over my head. Could it work? Could it really work?

"Jareth, you're right," I say, reaching over to take his hand in mine. I stroke his palm with my fingers. "I do need a little rest and recovery. And of course you can get the antidote without me. I mean, you're so big and strong and wonderful and all."

He looks at me, his eyes clouded with suspicion.

"And I'm so lucky to have you to take care of me," I continue. "You and Sunny. You're the best friends a vampire girl could have." I pause for dramatic effect, then add, "If only she were here right now. By my bedside. Keeping me company while you're away."

Jareth smiles, totally buying my act. Sucker. "Do you want me to send for her?" he asks. "I'd be happy to."

"Oh, would you, my darling?" I coo, looking up at him with round, innocent eyes. "I'd be forever grateful to see my sister in my time of need."

Jareth nods and pulls out his cell phone. I grin to myself. So he wants to play Daddy, does he? Well, get ready for a little *Parent Trap*.

14

God, my legs are cramped. Hiding in the airplane bathroom until we got over international waters seemed like a great idea at the time. Two hours later I'm not so sure. So I decide to take a chance. Hopefully we're far enough out that we won't have enough gas to turn back.

"Surprise!" I cry, jumping out in front of Jareth, who had been sleeping in the fully reclining leather seat of the coven's private jet. He jumps up with a start, his eyes wide as they fall upon me.

"Rayne!" he says, obviously flustered. "What—I mean how—I mean—"

"Why am I here, standing in front of you when I should

be under coven arrest? What am I thinking coming to England instead of seeing the shrink? How did I escape your big, burly vamp guards and manage to sneak onto a top-secret, high-security vampire plane?"

Jareth runs a hand through his hair. "Um, yes. I suppose all of the above."

"I'm here because you need me. I'm the Slayer. It's my job to find the antivirus and save the cheerleaders. And I'm not going to let anyone, including you, stop me from accomplishing my mission."

Jareth sighs, slumping down in his seat. "Of course you aren't," he says resignedly. "I should have known."

"And as to how I performed my Houdini act of disappearing—"

"You used Sunny. Of course," Jareth says, not allowing me my triumphant explanation. "You left your poor twin a prisoner in the coven while you stowed away on an impromptu trip to England. Did you make her dye her hair black, too?"

"Not permanently. And besides, she owed me. I covered her when she went to England last semester to go get the Holy Grail. Besides, she'll be fine. Like a vacation. Maybe they'll even allow Magnus in for a little conjugal visit. Not that she's made up her mind to have sex with him yet."

"I should have guessed it wasn't you when she called me

head off when I asked her if she needed anything to make her stay more comfortable."

"Really?" I raise an eyebrow. "Hmm. I told her to act mean and nasty. Guess she doesn't have it in her."

"And then there was that good-bye kiss . . ."

I stop short. "Wait! What? Sunny kissed you?" OMG, she kissed my boyfriend? I'm going to kill her. I mean, it's bad enough she accidentally stole Magnus from me to begin with. She's *so* not taking Jareth as well. Even if he is an overbearing pain in the ass. He's *my* overbearing pain in the ass.

"Oh yes. Extensive makeout session, actually," Jareth says with a thoughtful smile. "I was actually wondering if you'd been practicing, you were so improved—"

I grab the air phone off its receiver. "Oh, I am so having a word with her!"

Jareth starts laughing and grabs the phone from my hand. "I'm kidding!" he says, looking pleased with himself. "She didn't kiss me."

I narrow my eyes. "Are you sure? You're not just trying to cover for her, are you?"

"I wouldn't dream of it," Jareth says, still chuckling. "You know, Rayne, you're something else. You really are. I can't believe you managed to break out of the coven and onto the plane."

"The plane thing was easy. Just show up with a little bottle of blood laced with Ambien and the guard was down for the count."

"Well, you're creative, I'll give you that."

"So you're not mad?" I ask.

He sighs. "Not mad. Just . . . well, worried. It's not like I locked you up for no reason. I really do think it's for the best that you take some time off. Get used to being a vampire."

"I'm fine. Really I am. I just had a rough day. Too many people giving me a hard time. It happens to everyone."

"Everyone doesn't get into their car afterward and smash it into a guardrail."

"That was a total accident caused by lack of decent satellite radio stations. It had nothing to do with me being in a bad mood."

"Mmhm." Jareth doesn't sound too convinced. "You know, I still have half a mind to turn this plane around and drop you back off stateside."

"Oh, come on! Don't do that! I've been so looking forward to this trip. I want to meet all the English vampires. I mean, they're my peeps! And not in a weird, parasite-driven, Scott Westerfeld–novel type way, either. They're . . . well, they're my new family."

"Fine," Jareth relents. "But, please, I beg you, be on your best behavior on this trip. Remember we are representing our coven. The English vampires are very old and set in their ways. And we are their guests. We must be polite at all times. No flying into rages or telling them off. No matter what."

"Yes, yes, of course. God, what type of vampire do you think I am?"

Jareth grins wryly. "A Raynie type."

"And what, may I ask, is that?" I ask, hands on my hips.

"Unique. One of a kind." He grabs me and pulls me into an embrace. I allow myself to melt into his arms. He strokes my back. "Beautiful, stubborn, absolutely able to drive me crazy in two seconds flat."

"And?" I press.

"And the love of my unlife. Someone I never want to spend a day apart from."

"You'll never have to," I murmur, tilting my head upward. He smiles and leans down, kissing me softly. Mmm. I love this vamp of mine.

"I'm very glad to hear it."

15

After chatting for a while longer, we curl up on the plane's couch and fall asleep watching the surfing movie *Endless Summer*. (Jareth claims he only Netflixed it because he thought I wouldn't be along to complain and if he'd had any idea I'd be stowing away he would have rented the digitally remastered *Nightmare Before Christmas* collector's edition for sure.) I sleep well, for the first time in a while actually feeling somewhat content.

Sure I've still got problems. Cait's angry with me, Mandy's probably about to kick me off the squad, and my mother's ready to ship me off to my Vegas playboy of a dad so I won't harass her new boyfriend. Oh, and there's the car thing. Both she and Sunny are going to kill me when they find out I totaled it. (I sort of neglected to mention that to my twin when I was convincing her to trade places with me.) And, of course, my boyfriend thinks I need psychiatric intervention to cope with my vampire rage.

But cuddled up against Jareth, flying on a private jet to jolly old England where I will meet my undead brothers and sisters, find a werewolf antidote, and save the world again, I feel pretty darn good. Go ahead, life. Throw something at me. I, Rayne McDonald, can handle it.

I fall into a restful sleep, dreaming of Jareth and me walking into the English coven. It's decorated like some eighteenth-century ball and everyone curtsies when we enter. They announce us as Lord and Lady and we're seated at the head table, as guests of honor. One by one the English vamps approach us, bowing low and welcoming me to England. Vowing to spend their entire lifetimes, if necessary, to make sure I'm—

"Get up, get up, you sleepyhead!"

What the . . . ? The dream fades as an obnoxious cry invades my ears. I roll over, pulling the afghan over my head. But Jareth will have none of it. He grabs the blanket, ruthlessly ripping it from my body, and starts tickling me awake, which, if no one's ever done it to you, is by far the worst way of being woken up in the history of wake-up techniques.

"Wakey, wakey, eggs and bakey!" he says. Yes, these words actually come out of his mouth.

"Ugh. It's the middle of the night!" I protest, trying to squirm away from his fingers. "And we're vampires. We don't eat eggs or bakey." Not that it doesn't sound amazingly yummy right about now. But I'm so not going to admit that.

"I know," Jareth says. "Which is why I brought you some real breakfast." He holds out a squeeze bottle filled with red liquid.

"Ah, thanks!" I grab the bottle and suck through the straw greedily. Then I spit it out. "Argh!" I cry. "That's not my synthetic!"

Jareth sighs. "Sorry. But we don't have any synthetic on board. I didn't know you were coming, remember?"

I stare at the bottle. "So you gave me real blood? From a . . . real person?"

"That's usually where blood comes from, Rayne."

"But you know I don't drink it. How could you trick me like that?" I throw the bottle across the cabin in disgust.

"You're going to have to get over your aversion sooner or later. I thought now might be a good time to try."

"Thanks, but no thanks. Maybe they have some synthetic at the coven. I'm so not ready to be downing someone's vital bodily fluids."

"Rayne, you're a vampire," Jareth says. "That's what vampires do. You knew that before you turned. If you don't start drinking blood, you're going to waste away to nothing. And I'm sure the lack of sustenance has been one of the factors affecting your moods."

"No, *you're* one of the factors affecting my moods," I retort, annoyed as all hell that he tried to trick me like that. "Always being so pushy. I'll get there in my own time and I don't need to be rushed into something I'm not ready for."

Jareth sighs wearily, as if I'm the one being unreasonable.

"Fine. I won't bother you again," he says stiffly. "Just go get ready. We're due to be at the English coven in a half hour and I don't want to be late."

"Fine, I'll—" I stop short when I take a good look at him. "Hang on a second. You're going in that?" I ask, incredulous. "To the English coven?"

My vampire boyfriend, the once coolest Goth in the known universe, is currently dressed in an old faded Batman T-shirt and a pair of ripped jeans.

He shrugs. "Batman," he says, pointing to his chest. "Like me." He does a little flying imitation with his hands and grins. "I thought it was ironic."

Ironic? Ironic? "Dude! You can't show up to the coven looking like that!" I cry, panicked, my dreams of making a grand entrance going up in smoke. They'll laugh at us. They'll think I'm crazy for being at his side. They'll wonder why I didn't insist he change clothes.

"Why not?"

" 'Cause, well, 'cause," What am I supposed to say? 'Cause I'll be embarrassed to be seen with him? 'Cause the other vampires will think he's a total nerd and a half?

"Look, Rayne. It's not a big deal," Jareth reasons. "They're just vampires. Like the ones from our own coven. They won't care what we're wearing."

"They may not say they care, but they're going to judge us by what we look like. That's what people do. Do you want them to think you're some dork who just stepped out of Comic Con?"

"Frankly, my dear, I don't really care what they think. Rayne, we're not attending a fashion show. It's going to be a long night and I for one would like to be comfortable. What's the big deal?"

Argh! Did the blood virus somehow rob him of all cool-ness points along with his superpowers? First the beach, now stupid outfits. What's next? A sudden love for watching sports with his buddies while chugging beer and chowing on chips?

"What's wrong with you?" I demand, furious. "I mean, you used to be cool! You used to wear Armani and be all brooding and dark and stuff. Ever since we became blood mates it's like you've undergone a personality transplant. You've totally changed. Become a whole new person. In fact, half the time I feel like I don't even know you anymore."

Jareth's grin fades, replaced by a hurt expression, and I instantly regret what I said. "Well *you* certainly haven't changed." He sniffs. "You're your same nasty, bitter, angry old self who thinks the world owes her a favor. Sometimes I don't know why I bother."

I stare at him, my face hot with fury. I want to slap him, hurt him in some way. Make him feel as unhappy as I feel inside. But I force myself to suck in a breath before reacting. After all, this is my boyfriend. My blood mate. The one I love more than anyone in the world. Why am I so torn up inside? What's wrong with me?

"I know you're pissed off at the world, but I don't see why that means I have to bear the brunt of it. You've been nasty to me since school started," Jareth retorts. "And I'm sick of it. I'm not some doormat for you to walk over and ridicule and abuse because you've had a bad day. I'm sorry if me being happy for once in my life offends you so greatly."

"It's not that," I start, then stop. Is it that? Is that why I'm so mad at him? 'Cause he's happy and I'm not?

I burst into tears, furious at myself for being so messed up. Why can't I be a normal person? Like Sunny or someone. Why am I so angry and hateful? It's like I have this blackness in me. A burning pit of hatred that can't help but bubble up to the surface and lash out at those I love for no reason. I love Jareth. So much. And yet he's the one I'm most mean to.

You always hurt the ones you love . . .

"I just . . ." My voice cracks. "I just want them to like me," I admit, remembering the promise we made each other when we first got together. To share things. Even painful, hurtful things. "The other vampires. I want them to accept me as one of them."

Jareth's expression softens. He reaches over and puts a hand on my shoulder. "Raynie, luv," he says, "of course they'll like you. And acceptance has nothing to do with wardrobe, I swear." He pulls me close and strokes my head. "Sweetie, outside appearance doesn't matter. It's what's inside that counts," he says, again spouting self-helpisms.

"I know," I say, relenting. "You're right. I'm sorry."

But deep inside, I hope he's wrong. Because if what's inside is what really counts, I'm not sure I have much of a chance of impressing anyone.

16

We hop in a waiting limo and speed down the wrong side of the street to our destination. The bright lights of the big city of Manchester fall away and the darkness of the English moors provides an eerie backdrop to our nocturnal adventure. I peer out the window at the dark landscape unfolding in front of me as we race through the night.

"I wish we weren't just here on some mission," I comment to Jareth. "I'd love to check out the country someday."

"Well, we have all eternity," Jareth says, reaching over to take my hand in his. "We can definitely come back."

I smile, leaving the window and crawling over to his side of the limo. I put my head on his shoulder and snuggle close. He strokes my hand with his thumb in a way that gives me shivers.

"I'm sorry about before, Jareth," I murmur, feeling extremely comfy-cozy in his arms. "I don't know what came over me. I've just been getting so angry lately. It's kind of scary, really. When I get into these rages it's like I can't control my actions or what comes out of my mouth."

He kisses me on the top of my head. "You've gone through a tremendous amount of change in a short period of time. The stresses on you now are off the charts. It's enough to make anyone feel unsettled."

"It's just . . . and this sounds ridiculous when I say it out loud . . . I just thought once I became a vampire all my problems would . . . I don't know, go away." I shrug against him. "Stupid, huh?"

"Oh little one, you have much to learn," Jareth says. "But I promise to be there for you every step of the way."

"Really? You won't leave me?" I ask. "No matter what?"

"We're blood mates. I'm yours for eternity," he assures, shifting in his seat so we're face-to-face. He cups my chin in his hand, meeting my eyes with his own brilliant green ones. "I love you, Rayne McDonald."

I drop my eyes, unable to look at him. I feel so unworthy. His love is so strong and yet I'm so weak and pathetic. He gave up everything for me and I treat him like dirt. "I don't deserve you to love me," I whisper.

"What was that?" he asks, not catching my words.

"Um, nothing. Forget it." I look back up at him and force a smile. "I love you, too, Jareth. Always and forever."

He smiles and leans in to press his lips against mine. Slowly he caresses my mouth, coaxing me to open to him so he can explore me more thoroughly. Electricity tingles through my fingers and toes as we kiss, losing ourselves in one another, allowing all the stresses and problems to fade away. For this moment there are no werewolves or life-altering events that I must stop before it's too late. At this moment it is just me and my blood mate, giving, taking, comforting, loving.

We kiss for what seems like hours, exploring one another and discovering new depths of emotion and pleasure. And when the limo pulls to the side of the road and slows to a stop, it's way too early for me to want to part company.

We reluctantly stop kissing, pulling away slowly, as if industrial-strength magnets objected to us being apart. Jareth looks dazed and pleased. I'm sure I'm the same.

"Are you ready, my dear," he asks, "to meet the vampires?"

"Oh yes!" I say, excitement reverberating through me. "So ready!"

I jump out of the limo. We're parked in a circular driveway in front of the hugest mansion I've ever laid eyes on. It looks exactly like what you might imagine Madonna living in. A vast English estate with miles and miles (or as they say, kilometers and kilometers) of grassy lawn. I bet there're even stables here, filled with horses. Of course, they can only go night riding . . .

Jareth takes my hand in his and we walk up to the front doors, which sit between two pillars. He lifts up the large brass knocker (in the shape of a dragon) and lets it drop. It echoes a bang loud enough to wake the dead, which I guess is essentially what we're doing.

I squirm with excitement, hopping from one foot to the other, dying to see what the English vampires are like. I mean, these are my people. My blood relatives. These are the ones who will truly understand the real me. Who won't judge me because of what I look like or who I am. We'll have long talks and share laughs about pathetic mortals and their silly ways and maybe they'll even let me borrow some of their clothes. I bet they have marvelous—

Oh my God.

The door has swung open and on the other side stands Reese Witherspoon. Okay, not really Reese Witherspoon, but someone who looks a heck of a lot like Miss Legally Blonde. She looks about eighteen and is dressed like she's ready for her first day of prep school. White polo shirt, khaki pants with pleats in the front, even a pastel pink sweater tied around her neck.

This has to be the mortal the vampires are drinking from at dinner, right? There's no way this could be an actual—

"Jareth!" the girl cries, throwing her arms around my boyfriend. I notice she has a perfectly painted French manicure and a diamond tennis bracelet around her left wrist. "It's bloody good to see you, luv."

"Katie!" Jareth greets Miss Prep, hugging her back. "It's bloody good to be seen. How long has it been?" he asks, his English accent coming out in full force around another Brit.

"At least two hundred years," she says, pulling away from the hug and shaking a scolding finger. "Way too long."

My heart sinks. Two hundred years? There's no other explanation. She's a vampire. One of the English coven I'd been so looking forward to meeting. I can't believe it. I thought if anywhere there'd be cool, Gothy vamps, it would be in England. Evidently not so much.

Once again, I don't fit in.

Two more vampires, both looking like Blair and Serena from *Gossip Girl*, burst from the door. "Jareth!" they cry in unison.

"Ladies," my boyfriend says, debonairly. He bows to both of them. They giggle in response.

I narrow my eyes. Are they flirting with him? Don't they see me standing here, obviously his girlfriend? I glance down at myself, making sure I haven't somehow turned invisible or something. After all, not one of them has yet acknowledged my presence.

"You look great, Jareth," the blonde dressed in skinny jeans, slouchy boots, and a long cashmere sweater gushes, batting her obviously fake eyelashes at him. "As always."

"And what a funny shirt," adds the brunette, currently dressed in a lacy, baby blue camisole top and low-rise capris. "Batman! How utterly clever!"

Oh come on! You have *got* to be kidding me.

"Thank you," Jareth says, beaming. "I've always been quite fond of this shirt." He turns to me. "Rayne, here, on the other hand, thinks it could be a bit of a fashion faux pas."

Three pairs of eyes turn to stare at me. I'm given a complete once-over by each of them.

"*She* thinks it could be a fashion faux pas?" sniffs Katie. "The girl wearing black legwarmers with fishnets?"

I flush, suddenly wishing I could crawl under the pavement and die. I'd picked out this outfit especially to impress the English vamps and now it looked like it was going to be the object of ridicule.

"Is it Halloween already?" asks the blonde. "And here I thought that wasn't 'til October."

"Maybe she can't afford nice clothes," says the redhead. "I mean, look at that sweater she's wearing. Lots of rips and tears. In fact, I think it's only held together by safety pins."

"That's intentional," I mutter, looking down at the porch and kicking a floorboard with my toe. If only the porch would somehow magically open up and swallow me now.

"Ah! She's a Yank!" Katie squeals. "That explains it then."

"A vampire Yank. How utterly plebeian," sniffs Blondie.

I glance over at Jareth, waiting for him to defend me. But all he comes up with is "Katie, Susan, Elizabeth, this is Rayne. Rayne has only recently been reborn."

Recently reborn? Jeez. Why doesn't he just come right out and call me a vampire newbie or something?

The girls giggle, using his words as an excuse to bat their eyelashes at him a few more times. They are so transparent it's not even funny. No wonder Jareth moved to America and hasn't been back for a visit in two hundred years. I'd have stayed away for at least a thousand.

"Ah," says Elizabeth, the redhead. "She's young. That explains it then."

"Yes, the new ones always have this inexplicable urge to cater to Hollywood stereotypes," adds Katie. "I find it so amusing."

I glare at her. Amusing indeed. Well, maybe I find it *so amusing* that you all still have such sucky fashion sense even after a thousand years of practice.

I think this, but don't say it aloud. After all, I haven't forgotten Jareth's lecture on being on my best behavior. I've already let him down way too much. Got to prove I'm worthy of his trust. That he didn't make a mistake by not turning the plane around.

So I bite my tongue, even when Susan chimes in, "Imagine if all vampires wandered around dressed like they were dead. How utterly gloomy a way that would be to spend eternity."

"Too right." The girls nod in sync.

God, how long will we be roasting Rayne tonight? Don't you guys have coffins to climb into before sunrise? Maybe we could at least move off the porch and make fun of me inside the crypt?

I glance over at Jareth, who in turn avoids my stare. I've no doubt what he's probably thinking. Here I went on and on about his wardrobe not being cool enough. And it turns out it's me who ends up being the dork in this situation. He's probably laughing like crazy on the inside.

Not to mention he can't defend me in this case. As he said on the plane, we're guests here and we need to be on our best behaviors. Coven ambassadors from America. Besides, these vampires may be able to help us find the Lycans. And that's more important than my dignity at this juncture.

Just think of them like the cheerleaders, I tell myself. They're stupid and they don't know any better. But even the

Wolves are cooler than these vampires. And way more open-minded. In fact, now that I think of it, once I made the team, not one of them had a snide comment about my wardrobe. Even that day I forgot and wore fishnets under my uniform. And when I wore that skull belt to keep up my shorts, Shantel actually told me she thought it looked kind of cool. And Nancy asked if she could borrow my Manic Panic blue dye to paint streaks in her hair for spirit week.

I can't believe I'm standing at the entrance of one of the oldest vampire covens in the world and I'm missing the Oakridge High cheerleading squad.

"Shall we go in?" Jareth questions. Of course his suggestion is met with more giggles and gushing agreement. We step over the threshold and into a large, high-ceiled entryway, complete with a *Gone With the Wind* sweeping staircase and elaborate chandelier. I twirl around, forgetting the rude vampires for a moment, just taking it all in. The rich, jewel-toned walls, the elaborate gilded portraits of unidentified vampires. There are doors leading off in seemingly every direction, but not a single window. Guess they need to keep the place light-proof.

"This way," Katie says, ushering us to an elevator. She presses her thumb against a small gray pad and an LCD light beeps a green glow. Evidently this place has a pretty high-tech security system just like the coven back home. Don't want mortals breaking in during the day when everyone's asleep, I suppose. Stealing all their stupid designer clothes or something.

We step into the elevator and after Katie presses a button we shoot down underground. Deep underground. I feel a little like the mouse Mrs. Brisby in the *Secret of NIMH*. And, now that I think about it, these girls definitely remind me of rats.

A few minutes later, the elevator doors slide open and we enter a grand foyer. This place makes the aboveground area look like a peasant's shack. There are multiple chandeliers hanging at different lengths from the cathedral ceilings, beautiful paintings adorning gold-colored walls, and cozy couches around great big fireplaces. It looks like the lobby of the most elegant hotel in the world.

"Wow, this is beautiful," I remark, forgetting they all hate me and I'm trying to keep a low profile. "Totally cool."

"*Totally,*" mimics Susan. The other two stifle giggles.

A glare from Jareth convinces me to keep my mouth shut. Even though they're so asking for it, obviously.

Refusing to let them get me down, I walk over to one of the paintings to examine it closer. "Is this a da Vinci?" I ask in awe. I took art history two semesters in a row (okay, I flunked the first time around) and I definitely see the likeness to his other works, but don't recognize the painting.

"Yes," says Elizabeth. "One of his later works."

"It looks . . . new," I say, puzzled. It's then that I notice the Virgin Mary is wearing legwarmers and Jesus Christ has a Cabbage Patch Kid tucked away in the manger. "Uh, really new."

"Yes. That one's from his nineteen-eighties period," Katie says.

I laugh. "Ha, ha. Very funny."

"She's not joking," says Susan. "In fact, Leonardo painted some of his finest works between eighty-two and ninety-nine."

"Dude, I hate to break it to you, but the guy's been dead a thousand—" I stop. "Wait a second. Is he a . . . ?"

"Italian Renaissance Coven Number 109," Katie recites. "Of course now all his works are only found in private collections like this. We can't let mortals know he's still painting."

Wow. I can't believe Leonardo da Vinci is a vampire. I wonder how many other ancient celebrities are still kicking it underground these days.

"We vampires believe that the masters' works were far too important to simply bow to this mortal coil," Katie further explains. "So we turned most of them into vampires. Musicians like Mozart, painters like Michelangelo, writers like Dante. They still produce amazing art to this day. Though Mozart's been in a real tiff lately after someone leaked his new concerto over the Internet before its official release date. He's so against Internet piracy."

"Oh, and Michelangelo's completely given up the chiseling statues out of stone thing now that Pixar's got him on staff for their new David and Goliath flick," adds Susan. "Of course we all told him the censors wouldn't go for the no-fig-leaf look in a G-rated pic, but does he listen?"

"Oh, and Dante?" Elizabeth says. "He's given up *Divine Comedy* to work on the situational type. Though I'm not sure the *Everybody Hates Satan* pilot he's producing is going to get picked up by the network. It just seems a little bleak for a sitcom, what with all those tortured people in various circles of hell and all."

"Wow. Just . . . wow." I say. I heard rumors there were a lot of famous vamps walking the earth, but I had no idea they were so busy. And here I am all concerned about graduating high school. I wonder what I can accomplish with immortality.

Katie clears her throat. "So, if we're done with Art History 101, shall we retire to the library for drinks?" she asks. "After all, we have a lot of catching up to do."

"Sounds lovely," Jareth says. "Lead the way. Of course it's been ages since I've visited."

"Yes, dreadfully too long," coos Elizabeth, putting an arm around my boyfriend's shoulders. Susan flanks him on the other side, wrapping her arm around his waist. I grit my teeth and claw at my palms and remind myself this is only for one night. If I can just put up with their antics now, Jareth will think I'm a wonderful, patient, open-minded person and he'll be glad that I'm his blood mate for all eternity.

If I can survive the night.

Katie leads the way, down the foyer and through a set of double doors and into a cozy library. The place is floor-to-ceiling books, all hardbound and embossed with gold lettering. I'm dying to know what they're about, but it seems rude to just start pulling out volumes. Not to mention if there's some secret bookcase door that's hinged on the right book being pulled out (like always happens in old English movies) I don't want to accidentally trigger it. *Trés* embarrassing.

We sit down on comfy leather couches and Katie rings a bell. A moment later a servant-type appears. He's old, probably in his late sixties, with thinning white hair. He's dressed in a tuxedo and walks with a slight limp. Definitely not a vampire. Interesting that they have human servants here. Do they double as blood donors, I wonder?

"Charles, go into the cellar and get us a vintage O negative," requests Elizabeth.

"Ooh, good choice," chimes in Susan. "Get the one from Marie Antoinette. After all, this is a night of celebration to have our dear brother Jareth back from the United States."

The servant bows and exits the library.

"Uh, Marie Antoinette?" I question, a little nervously.

"We have some very expensive bloods in our possession," explains Katie. "Bottled and stored until we decide to indulge."

"You're serving us blood of Marie Antoinette? Like, the real person? The queen of France?" Wow, that's crazy.

"Would you rather we let you eat cake?" quips Susan.

I roll my eyes at her lame joke. "But I thought, like, she was executed during the French Revolution. Is she a vampire, too?"

"No. She's dead. Duh. You can't really go back from being beheaded. And besides, how would we have a bottle of her blood lying around if she were undead and well?"

I guess that's true. "So then how . . . ?"

"Vampires assisted with that rebellion," explains Susan. "Did you really think that the peasants could have toppled a monarchy with no assistance? Please. They were too busy picking lice off their unbathed bodies."

"Royal blood is always extra rich," adds Elizabeth. "Good diet and all. So when each monarch was beheaded, there was a vampire bottler on hand to collect the blood."

"Wow, that's, um, fascinating?" Actually I think it's really, really disgusting, but I'm still trying to cling to manners here.

Katie smiles smugly. "We here at the Blood Coven of Northern England have a pretty extensive blood cellar. We've got a couple of bottles of Henry the Eighth, Shakespeare.

Even a half bottle of Jack the Ripper, if you're in the mood for something adventurous."

I'm pretty sure I'll never be that adventurous. I can't even stomach fresh blood, never mind the bottled bodily fluids of a serial killer from the nineteenth century. And I'm pretty sure I'm not up for any French queen blood tonight either. Hopefully they'll decide it's far too expensive to waste on a newbie Yank Goth vamp and I won't have to make a scene by turning it down.

"In any case," Jareth says. "Rayne and I are here on official business. We are looking for a Lycan community somewhere in this vicinity. They may have infected some of our local townspeople and we need to find out if there's an antidote for the disease."

"Try the town of Appleby," suggests Susan. "Last I heard there was a Lycan pack living there. Order of the Gray Wolf, I believe they're called."

"They live in towns?" I ask, surprised. I don't know why but I figured they all hung out in dark, dank caves or something. You know, being werewolves and all. "Even though on full-moon nights they go all beastie and stuff?"

"The pack is not immortal like vampires, but as a whole they've existed for thousands of years," says Elizabeth. "They have learned the art of controlling their metamorphoses."

"Meta—?"

"Their change to wolf form. They don't rely on the pull of the moon. They can change at will and control their actions in their feral forms."

"Ah, handy. And much better for the other townspeople."

"Go to the Tavern of the Moon and inquire there. That's where the pack spends most of its time," says Susan. "Ask for a man named Lupine. He's the alpha wolf, leader of the pack. Tell him we sent you. He should be able to help."

"What I don't understand though is how your local townspeople came to be infected," says Katie. "I mean, Lycans are much like vampires. Very selective in adding members to the pack. They don't just take anyone. In fact, most people are only Lycans through birth. And even if they were turned for some reason, they would never, ever be sent off on their own—unprepared and untrained. It doesn't make any sense."

"I agree. Which is why we need to seek out this order and find out what happened," Jareth says. "Otherwise these lone wolves may have to be put to sleep." He turns to me. "Tomorrow we will head over to Appleby to see what we can learn from this Order of the Gray Wolf."

I nod. "Sounds like a plan."

The servant re-enters the library with what looks like a bottle of wine and five glasses. He sets the glasses down on a side table and uncorks the blood. He pours a small amount of the red liquid into each glass.

I swallow hard and my hands start shaking. I shove them under my thighs. The smell, even from where I am, is almost overwhelming. Rich, spicy, even better than the fresh blood I smelled on Cait. And I'm starving, too, having not drunk a synthetic in almost twenty-four hours. But if I don't drink now they're really going to think I'm a poseur.

What to do? What to do?

The girls all raise their glasses. "To Jareth," says Katie with a seductive smile. "And the hope that in the future his visits will be longer and more frequent."

They all drink. I stare down at my goblet.

Just take a sip, Rayne. It won't hurt you.

Ugh. I can't do it. I just can't bring myself to slurp up the blood of an eighteenth-century monarch. I swallow hard and make the decision to come clean. Who knows, maybe they'll miraculously understand and feel a sense of empathy for me and my blood phobia. Not likely, but I'm desperate for a drink.

"Uh, you guys don't have any, uh, synthetic around here, do you?"

"A what?" queries Elizabeth. "A synthetic?"

My face burns. "You know, like fake blood. It delivers the proper nutrients, but is made in a lab."

The three vampires look at me and then each other, bursting into laughter.

"Why on earth would you want that?"

"Especially when you've got one of the top bloods in the world sitting in front of you!"

I grit my teeth, my stomach churning with embarrassment. I never should have said anything. Should have told them I wasn't hungry or something. Anything but admit I don't exactly drink real blood on a regular basis.

"I just do, okay?" I say.

But the girls aren't listening to me anymore. They've found another reason to put me down and they're relishing it. First my clothes, then my American accent, now my aversion to blood. They're having a field day at my expense.

"A vampire who doesn't drink blood."

"Jareth, wherever did you pick up this girl? She's precious!"

"They're definitely scraping at the bottom of the barrel for new recruits these days!"

"And she's your blood mate, Jareth? Bad luck, luv. Bad luck indeed."

"What kind of vampire are you, anyway?" giggles Elizabeth. "A vegetarian? Do you suck tomatoes dry?"

I squeeze my hands into fists. Why do I have to take this abuse? So we're in their coven. Whatever. That doesn't mean I deserve this rude behavior. I've been nothing but polite to them since I walked in the place. I answered them respectfully, I put up with their abuse. I even kept my mouth shut when they openly poked fun at me.

But now I, Rayne McDonald, have had enough.

"What kind of vampire am I?" I ask, rising from my seat. I reach in my back pocket and rip out my stake. The one I carved last semester when training to be a slayer. It catches the candlelight and flashes a white glow, illuminating the suddenly freaked out, pale white faces of my new friends.

"I," I say, holding the stake out in front of me, leaping to battle stance, "am a vampire vampire slayer."

17

"Well, that was a bloody genius move, that was," Jareth proclaims a few minutes later as we walk down the driveway, escorted by a big, burly, human guard. It's started to rain (damn English weather!) and my hair is already plastered to my head.

"Sorry," I mutter. It's dark. I can't see where I'm going and I've just stepped into a puddle with my definitely not waterproof ballet flats. I'm not a happy camper. "But they were totally asking for it. I've never met such a catty group of women in all my life. Sue me for losing my temper."

"Losing your temper is one thing. Brandishing a wooden stake while standing in the center of one of the most prestigious vampire covens in the western hemisphere is quite another," Jareth says. "You're lucky I was able to talk them out of executing you on the spot. I can assure you, they've snuffed out vampires for far more minor indiscretions than yours."

"Oh, whatever. It's not like I was going to stake them. I just wanted to scare them a bit. Make them see I wasn't some tool to be trifled with."

"Well, they certainly are not trifling with you now, are they? And I'd wager a thousand pounds they won't trifle with you ever again. A little advice, my dear: When you're planning on living for the rest of eternity, it's not such a great idea to alienate your fellow vamps your first year out."

I sigh. "I know, I know. I'm sorry. But you gotta admit, they were totally rude and nasty to me. And by the way, what's with you just standing by and letting them make fun of me, huh? Some blood mate you are."

Jareth sighs. "We weren't there on a social call, Rayne. We needed information from them. Being polite and excusing some bad behavior was the only way to go about getting it. You've got to toughen up. Get a thicker skin. You're far too sensitive."

I open my mouth to respond, but am interrupted by the security guard. We've reached the gate and he's requesting we step through. Leave the premises, don't come back, all that jazz. He presses a button and the wrought-iron monstrosity creaks open. We have no choice; we walk outside the perimeter. A moment later the gate clangs shut behind us.

I look around, squinting through the fog and rain. The dirt road leading up to the mansion stretches endlessly in each direction with no other houses in sight. We're in the middle of nowhere.

"Where do we go now?" I ask, my teeth chattering. I didn't dress for the cold, rainy weather, that's for sure. And all my baggage is still in chez vampire.

"I haven't the slightest idea." Jareth turns around, scanning the landscape. "I told the limo driver not to come back until tomorrow and we're miles from any sort of civilization."

"I can call a cab . . ." I rummage into my coffin purse to pull out my cell phone. But as I flip it open, I suddenly remember we're in another country. And sad to say, Mom hadn't seen a reason to sign up her teenage daughter to an international calling plan. Go figure. "Or not." I sigh.

I'm beginning to realize that perhaps I *was* a bit hasty whipping out my stake in front of the English coven. After all, I'd rather be called every name in the book than spend a night out in the wilds of the northern English moors.

But as they say, hindsight is 20/20 and I'm SOL.

The rain starts coming down harder. Pelting me from all directions, the wind whipping through my hair and battering my face. I hug my arms against my chest in a desperate attempt to get warm, looking over at Jareth, praying he has a plan.

Without saying anything, Jareth starts walking down the dirt road, taking long strides, as if he's trying to get some distance between himself and me. Not that I blame him. I'd be mad at me, too. Still, we're stuck in this together and holding a grudge is not going to help matters. I scramble to keep up, all the while keeping my head down to avoid being blinded by the rain.

A few minutes later we come to a small, withered barn sitting a few yards back from the road. It's run-down and weather-beaten, but to me at this moment it looks like a five-star hotel. Jareth motions to me to follow him as he pushes open the door and heads inside.

I blink a few times, my eyes adjusting to the darkness as Jareth closes and bolts the barn door behind us. There're a few empty stalls, a loft filled with musty-smelling hay. Some unidentifiable farm instruments lined up against one wall. I hope there aren't any mice or rats that hang out here.

"Well, it's not the Ritz, but it's dry," Jareth says with a shrug. "Should tide us over 'til morning when the limo comes back to retrieve us."

He breaks apart a bale of hay and fashions a small straw bed out of it. Then he shrugs out of his jacket and hangs it on one of the lower rafters. Next he takes off his shirt. God, he looks good with no shirt on. Such washboard abs. I wish he wasn't pissed at me. I'd so go over and run my fingers up and down them if I thought I could get away with it.

"Here," he says stiffly, holding out the shirt. "It's a lot dryer than what you've got on."

He's right. I hadn't the foresight to wear a coat and my sweater is dripping wet. "But what about you? Won't you freeze?"

He shrugs. "Once you're a vampire for over a thousand years you get used to different climates. Better you take it."

I almost believe him. That is until I catch him suppressing a shiver when he thinks I'm not watching. How sweet is that? He literally gave me the shirt off his back. Even though he's mad at me.

He turns his back and I slip off my sweater and out of my bra, then pull on the Batman shirt. It's amazing how easy it is to become a fashion victim when you're freezing to death.

Jareth collapses on the hay bed and curls into a fetal position. Seeing my opening, I scamper over to join him and lie down, trying to cuddle against him. Unfortunately a stiff plank would be more giving than my boyfriend at the moment. And a moment later he rolls over, giving me the cold shoulder.

I scowl at his back. So it's like that, is it? Shirt charity aside, he's still mad.

"Wow, I never thought I'd spend my first night in England in a barn," I say, giving it one more attempt. Maybe I can talk him out of being mad at me. It's worked before. "Pretty crazy."

"Especially when you consider we could have lain on a four-thousand-dollar bed with Egyptian cotton sheets tonight," Jareth remarks with more than a bitter note in his voice. Not exactly the reaction I'd hoped for.

"Geez, give it a rest," I grumble, annoyed he can't just move on. This could be a romantic adventure and all he can do is complain. "So I made a mistake. Do I have to be reminded every five seconds?"

Jareth shifts, pulling away from my hold. He stands up, paces the barn a few times, then turns to me. "You know, it's awfully funny," he says, and I can tell by his tone that I'm not going to find what he says next the least bit amusing. "Here you were so worried about *me* embarrassing *you*."

I groan and give up. He's obviously not going to do the whole sun setting on your anger thing, so why should I bother?

"Whatever," I say, rolling my eyes and turning my back to him. "I still think your shirt is stupid."

When I wake up the next morning at first I'm not quite sure where I am. Then I smell the hay and see the pitchforks and it all comes back to me. By the light of day the whole thing seems so dumb. Why had I opened my big mouth and told the vampires I was a slayer? I mean, sure, they were rude, but

I was used to rudeness, right? Pretty much everyone I know has been rude to me at one time or another.

Including Jareth.

I sit up and scan the barn, finally locating my boyfriend on the polar opposite end of the barn. As far away from me as humanly (vampirely?) possible. Sigh. I wonder if he'll forgive me anytime soon or spend the day holding a grudge. I can't believe we're in yet another fight. Lately that seems all we ever do. And I can't break up with him. He's my blood mate for eternity. Not that I want to. I love him. I just don't know why we can't seem to get along anymore. It sucks.

The rain has ended and I can hear birds chirping outside. I walk over to the barn door and push it open, squinting in the early morning sunshine. The air is crisp, cool. I wrap my arms around my chest, hugging myself for warmth, wishing I had my luggage and access to my wool coat.

I couldn't see much last night but today I realize the barn is sitting on miles and miles of wild English countryside. Rolling green, grassy hills, stone fences, blossoming wildflowers, and wandering sheep. It looks like something out of a postcard. Down the road I see a beautiful lake, the sun catching the water and making it sparkle.

"I always thought England was the most beautiful country in the world," Jareth says, coming up behind me.

"I'm glad I'm getting to see it," I say, turning around, ready to kiss and make up. But Jareth doesn't look very interested. He sidesteps me and walks out into the open air. I sigh. This is going to be a long day.

I realize at the very least I should apologize. Grovel and hope he'll forgive me. "Look, I'm sorry about last night, Jareth. That was a really dumb move. Even for me."

"Yes. It was indeed," he says coldly. "And one that will likely cost us for centuries to come."

I frown. Here I thought he was going to say, "Don't worry, no big deal, I can't help but love your free-spirited ways, Raynie baby." He must be really pissed. Either that or I really screwed up big-time. Just great.

"So now what?" I ask, resigning myself to his attitude. After all, what choice do I have?

"The limo should be waiting for us. We'll walk back to the coven and flag the driver down. The vampires will be fast asleep and won't notice we're back."

"And what about our luggage?"

"We'll see if the driver can convince the guard to retrieve it for us. Otherwise we'll have to stop at a shop and buy a few more things."

The limo driver is easy to spot and he doesn't ask questions as to why we're outside the gate and not walking down from the coven. Or why we're all rumpled and smelly and have hay sticking out of our clothing and hair. He goes to the gatehouse and returns with our bags a few minutes later. I unzip my duffel and check to make sure it's all there. I so did not want to lose that one-of-a-kind, genuine seventies se-quined tube top I found thrifting last spring. Luckily, these vampires don't have enough alternative fashion sense to un-derstand what a valuable article of clothing they could have confiscated.

My stake, on the other hand, does not seem to be among my possessions anymore. Great. Now I'll have to carve a new one from scratch.

"So how are we going to get the townspeople to tell us about the Lycan pack?" I ask, settling down into my black leather seat and pulling the door closed behind me. Did I mention I love riding in limos? My stiff back from my night on the barn floor is feeling better already. "I mean, we can't just go into that bar and start asking random people if they've seen any werewolves lately, can we?"

"Actually," Jareth says thoughtfully, "that's exactly what we're going to do."

"What?" I stare at him, incredulous. "But that's stupid. They're going to think we're total freaks. They'll run us out of town. Even if they do know where the pack is, why would they tell a couple of tourist types?"

"Because we're tourists with the vampire scent."

Ah, the vampire scent. I'd forgotten about that. Each vampire gives off pheromones that make us irresistible to op-posite sex humans. Of course this can become very irritating after the novelty wears off and you've already gotten out of a speeding ticket or two. I mean, teacher giving you an A on a test because he's in love with you = good. Random guy coming up off the street and licking you = not so good. So from day one we're taught to control the vampire scent. Push it down, deep inside. And if that doesn't work, we have these special deodorant sprays that keep it from sweating out our pores. In fact, until Jareth brought it up just now, I'd about forgotten I even possessed the vampire scent.

"You very clever, Old Master," I quip, *Kung Fu*–style. "Young Grasshoppa have much to learn."

Jareth laughs, but it sounds forced. Why am I even bothering? "Here's what we'll do," he says, back to business. "You'll go down to the pub and do one walk around the perimeter. Let everyone catch a whiff of you. Then, when you've got the entire bar's attention, go to the center of the room and find a table to sit down at. If it works, you should have male company in three seconds flat. Once you've got their attention, tell them you're a graduate student looking to study Lycan for your thesis and you were told there's a pack that lives here."

"And you think they'll tell me?"

"Under the spell of the vampire scent they'd tell you a lot more."

I laugh. "I don't think I want to know more."

"Just please, Rayne," Jareth says, his eyes serious. "Whatever you do, *don't* tell them you're a slayer."

"Yes, yes. I mean, duh. No kidding."

"Well, sorry for mentioning it, but I would have assumed it was 'duh, no kidding' last night, too. You know, when we were surrounded by actual vampires?"

I grit my teeth. He's so going to hold this over my head for eternity, isn't he? "Jareth, I made a mistake. I said I was sorry, okay? Can we drop it now?"

"Rayne, you can't just laugh your way out of this. What you did was not cute, not funny, and not not a big deal. You were representing your coven there. And international vampire relations are vitally important to our coven's survival. Did you know they could actually vote us out of the council, just for having a slayer in our ranks? We could lose all our rights and privileges as a member of the consortium. You obviously don't seem to grasp the seriousness of what you did."

I feel like crying. I can't believe how stupid I was. To let my big mouth get the best of me again. No wonder no one wants to be my friend. I'm such a loser.

"I'm sorry," I say, choking on the words. "I didn't know."

Jareth shakes his head, as if he's weary of the world. "Just forget it," he mutters. "There's nothing that can be done anyway. Vampires can come later. Right now we need to concentrate on the wolves."

18

The village of Appleby is small and quaint. There's an ancient castle in the center of town, a crumbling almshouse that's been transformed into an old folks' home, narrow, cobblestone streets, and plenty of pubs and little shops. It'd drive me crazy to actually live in a small town like this, but it's really cool to visit.

We check into Appleby Manor, a charming little hotel on the outskirts of town, and get ready for our wolf recon. As I change clothes in the bathroom, Jareth preps me for the thousandth time about what I need to do. About a half hour later we head down to the Tavern of the Moon. Even though it's not quite noon, there's a good number of men hanging out at the bar, having a few pints, watching the football game. (That's soccer to you Americans, though it makes more sense for them to call their game football, seeing as they use their feet a heck of a lot more than American football players do . . .)

Jareth takes a seat at the back end of the pub and I prepare to make my grand entrance. I walk down alongside the bar, watching them watch me in the mirror on the wall. One by one they swivel in their barstools and stare at me and my sequined tube top and micromini skirt. (Jareth thought my outfit was total overkill, but by the looks on the men's faces, he was so wrong.) I smile coyly as I turn around to face them. Several are staring with their mouths wide open. One looks like he's literally about to drool.

"Hi, boys," I purr. "What's a girl gotta do around here to get a drink?"

A mad dash to be the first to buy me a pint ensues. A few men jump off their barstools and offer me their seats. I take a stool, pulling it away from the bar so I can see all the men at once. I sit down, crossing my legs. I'm very Sharon Stone, *Basic Instinct*, though I'm definitely wearing panties. (So not going to pull a Britney for this crowd.) One man hands me a pint of lager. I take a long sip. As a vampire I can't really get drunk, but I bet I look impressive draining my glass in one long gulp.

"So," I say. "I have a question."

"We likely have an answer, ma'am," says one of the guys.

"And if not, we can find out."

"Yes, ask away, beautiful lady."

"Oh, you boys are so sweet," I coo. "Very well then. But I warn you, it may sound a bit strange."

"It won't, miss," says a burly guy at the far end. "Don't worry about that."

"Okay," I say, reaching into my purse and pulling out a cigarette. I slowly light the tip and take a drag. (I know, I know, I totally said I was quitting. But I'm a vampire. I can't exactly die of lung cancer. So I think once in a while it might be okay to light up—especially when I'm doing everything I can to channel sexy, bad girl Rayne.) "I'm looking for a pack of wolves."

The men stare at me and then at each other. Some wear complete poker faces while others start sweating a little.

"Wolves?" the tallest man says. He has shoulders the size of a linebacker's, pads on. "I'm sure out in the woods you can find—"

"Oh, silly boy, you know I'm not talking about common, everyday wolves," I chide him. "I mean, what do you take me for? Some stupid woman?"

Head shakes all around. No, of course they don't. At this moment they see me as Venus herself. I should use this vampire scent thing more often.

"What I'm looking for, boys," I say, "are Lycans." I pause for dramatic effect. "Do you know where I can find a pack of Lycans living in this town?"

"Find 'em?" pipes in a skinny man from the back. "You already have 'em, missie."

Rumbling conversation breaks out between the men. There's obviously some argument about whether that little fact should have been revealed. I'm, of course, delighted. This was easier than I thought. As much as I hate the English vampires, they totally hooked us up with the right location.

I glance over at the men. Could they really be Lycan? The pack I'm looking for? They look so normal. So working-class Englishman. But then the cheerleaders aren't exactly sprouting fangs and fur on their non–full-moon days, either.

"So you all are . . . ?"

A consensus seems to have been reached and a big, burly man to my right steps forward, puffing out his chest in pride. "We're all Lycans. The lot of us."

I smile. "How lucky for me to have stumbled upon you."

"Indeed," the man says. "I am Lupine, alpha of the Order of the Gray Wolf, at your service."

Does one shake hands with a werewolf? Or do they, I don't know, sniff butts to get to know one another? Ew, I so don't want to go there. I decide to try the handshake. Luckily Lupine shakes back, making no sudden move for my ass. "So you're wolves, but you live in town as men?" I query. I've got to warm them up a bit before I tell them what I really want.

"Of course. Don't believe the stories you read in horror novels, miss. Most Lycans are prominent members of their communities. We can control our shape-shift and are completely in control of our actions when in feral form."

I think back to the cheerleaders and the havoc they wreaked on my town. Definitely not exhibiting the control thing there.

"What about during the full moon? Don't you go all crazy then?"

The men laugh. "Only the newbies," they explain. "And we keep them under lock and key until we can train them to control their instincts."

"The full moon is an easy pull to resist, once you've had some training," Lupine explains. "It's the desire to mate that can bring out your inner wolf, even in the most disciplined among us." He gestures to a man at the back of the bar. "For example, look at John over there. He's starting to change right now, just from looking at you."

I glance over at John, who's standing behind the others. He's sprouted some gray hair on his chest and white fur is sticking out of his ears. I watch, fascinated, as his nose seems to elongate like Pinocchio's, right before my eyes.

His face turns crimson as he realizes we're all staring at him. "Uh, I've, uh, got to go see a man about a dog," he mutters, turning and fleeing the bar.

The men break out into laughter, slapping each other on the back.

"John's always been a bit of a lady's wolf," Lupine says with a chuckle.

"So he . . . ?"

"Yes, lass. Basically, you see, when we get horny, we get, well, hairy!"

Um, ewh. I wonder what the womenfolk think of that. Though, I guess they're probably in the same fuzzy boat. Of course, this would mean it's a lot harder to hide the fact that your partner just isn't doing it for you anymore.

Sorry, dear, I just can't seem to get hairy tonight.

Don't worry, dear. It happens to all wolves once in a while.

One of the men leans in to sniff me. (No, not my butt, thank goodness.) "You're not human yourself, lass," he proclaims. "Your blood smells funny."

Now it's my turn to blush. Should I tell them the truth? I guess it's okay. After all, these guys just admitted they regularly howl at the moon. A little fang will seem like nothing to them.

"I'm a vampire," I confess. "Just turned last spring."

They look at me, wide-eyed and interested. "A vampire, eh?" says one. "I've never met a real one before."

"Do you sleep in a coffin?"

I laugh. "No, I have a room at Appleby Manor."

"Can you not see your own reflection?"

"Do you think my hair would look this good if I couldn't?"

"What about crosses? Do they burn you like fire?"

"Totally. And I'm really grossed out by garlic. But I never liked that before my conversion either, so no big loss."

"Do you die if someone stakes you through the heart?"

I groan. "Jeez, guys, give it a rest. I'm a vampire, not a freak show. And besides, you guys are werewolves. Do silver bullets work? Do you howl at the moon? Is the *American Werewolf in London* based on any of your kin?"

They laugh and slap me on the back. "Touché, vampire lass," one says. "Touché."

"So one more question," says Lupine. "Why is a Yank vampire like you looking for Lycans in our humble bar?"

"Well, I'm glad you asked," I say. "Do you remember a group of American girls coming this way last summer? They would have been here for some cheerleading competition."

The men groan in sync. "Can't forget them," says one. "Me ears were ringin' from the blasted noise they made for near three weeks after they left."

I laugh. "Yup, that would be them," I say. "Well, they're now back in Massachusetts, of course, but they've . . . changed."

"What do you mean?"

"Um, simply put, I think they're werewolves."

The men erupt in concerned murmurs. I wait patiently, lighting another cigarette.

Finally Lupine speaks. "That's impossible," he says.

I shrug. "Impossible or not, I'm telling you the truth. And this is the one place where they could have become infected."

"But we haven't turned a wolf in more than five hundred years," Lupine says. "Bringing in new mouths to feed would be counterproductive. It would destroy the pack. The only way you can enter the Order of the Gray Wolf is to be born into it."

I scratch my head. That doesn't make any sense. If they don't turn people into werewolves, how was the squad infected?

"Is there any way there could be someone outside your pack who could have done an unauthorized bite or something?"

The men talk amongst themselves again. "What about the Lone Wolf?" I hear one ask.

"The what?"

"There was a boy who challenged Lupine, our alpha," the man explains. "He had delusions of grandeur. Decided he wanted to take over the pack. Of course he was defeated." The men all look gratefully at Lupine, who I imagine was the one who kicked this guy's ass. "And sent away, tail between his legs."

"But as he left, he vowed revenge. Said he would start his own pack and eventually destroy us."

"Perhaps he found your girls and decided to make them his mates."

Lupine squeezes his hands into fists. "I knew I should not have let him leave alive."

I'm beginning to get a sick, excited feeling in my stomach. "That's got to be it. He must have somehow bitten all the cheerleaders while they were here for their tournament."

"Kiss 'em is all he'd have to do," explains a bearded guy in the front. "Lycanthropy is spread through saliva."

I remember Shantel talking about the party they all went to. How they got so drunk they didn't remember how they got home.

"But why wouldn't he keep them here in England? Why let them go back to America?"

"He's weak. Not born to be an alpha. He may have not been able to stop them. But you can be sure he's sending them telepathic messages. And once he gains more strength, he will call to them. And they will come."

"The situation is grave indeed," says Lupine, his yellow-ish eyes squinting in worry. "Untrained wolves running around. They could cause serious problems when the moon is full."

"Yeah, they already are. That's why I'm here. We have to figure out a way to cure them. Is there one?" I cross my fingers, praying for an affirmative answer.

Luckily Lupine nods. "There is an antidote," he says. "When our cubs reach maturity we give them the choice. Stay with the pack or live the rest of their days as a human.

Those who choose humanity are doused with antidote and sent out into the world, never to return."

Hope sparks inside me. "Great! I was hoping you'd say that!" I exclaim. "Do you have any to spare that I can take back to America?"

"We can make some up for you, not a problem. Just takes a little of the old secret ingredient," Lupine says. The men all chuckle and I wonder what joke I'm missing out on.

"Secret ingredient?"

"Alpha wolf piss," explains Lupine.

I stare at him. "Um, ew?"

The men laugh.

"Don't worry, luv," says Lupine. "We distill it and by the time it's in antidote form it's only one part of a million. You won't even be able to smell it."

"Oh-kay. I trust you," I say. Actually it's a bit amusing to imagine feeding the cheerleaders wolf piss. "So how's it administered?"

"Topically. Just let it seep through the skin."

"That sounds easy enough."

"Not really. You see, it can only be applied when they're in wolf form."

"Oh." Yes, I can see where that would be a bit more challenging. What am I supposed to do? Wait 'til homecoming and then try to trap them all in the same room? Get out the old Super Soaker and blast them all with it once they start growing claws and teeth? If it doesn't work right away I'll have some pretty angry, deadly wolves on my ass.

I shake my head. I'll think of something. The important thing now is to get the antidote.

"So when can you have it made?" I ask.

"Give us 'til tomorrow morning," says Lupine. "We'll have it for you by then."

"Great!" I exclaim. "Thank you, guys. You're really helpful."

"Not a problem. We're sorry this happened to your friends. When we find Lone Wolf we will definitely take him out so this does not happen again."

"One more question," I say. "A few of our football players have been missing since the whole incident. Do you think it's possible they were . . . eaten?"

The men look at one another, then shake their heads. "Unlikely," they say. "Are these boys attractive to the bitches?"

I know he means female dogs, but I kinda like the innuendo. "Sure. In fact, one of them is the boyfriend of the cheerleader."

"Then it's doubtful they ate them. More likely they're presenting them as a gift to Lone Wolf, their alpha. Subservient males to put under his control. A rogue wolf like him would like weak, human males because it will not challenge his dominance."

"I see," I say. Hmm, I wonder how I can find out where they stashed the boys. "Thanks, guys. You were really helpful. I'll come back in the A.M. to get the antidote."

"Not a problem, vampire," says Lupine. "Perhaps someday our kinds will meet again. You are always welcome to howl with us."

I grin. I'm so not going to turn away from this chance. "Arrroooooo!"

19

B ack at our hotel room, I fill Jareth in on all I've learned from the Lycans.

"So all we have to do is wait 'til tomorrow morning and we'll have our antidote," I inform him. "Of course I have no idea how we're going to douse them with the stuff, seeing as they have to be in wolf form for it to work. But we'll cross that bridge when we come to it, I guess, right? In any case, I did good, huh? Mission accomplished. And I didn't even piss them off. Not a single wolf raised his hackles at me. You'd have been so proud."

I pause for breath, hoping to get at least some sort of kudos for all my hard work. I look over at Jareth. He's staring at a hotel painting on the wall, so intently that if I didn't know better I'd say it had the secrets of the universe embedded between brushstrokes.

"Jareth?"

He shakes his head and turns to face me. "You did well," he says. "I'm sure Slayer Inc. will be very pleased with your work."

I sigh. Who gives a care about Slayer Inc.? I want him to say *he's* pleased with my work. Geez, the guy can really hold a grudge.

I square my shoulders, determined to break him from his bad mood. I've done it before. In fact, it's my specialty. The Get Jareth in a Good Mood and Make Him Forget He's Mad at Me twelve-step program. I've done it so many times I should be giving seminars at this point. Though, of course, I seem to be the only one able to piss him off frequently enough to warrant a training session.

"So we should celebrate, don't you think? Maybe go out on the town, tonight? I mean, sure it isn't much of a town, but it could be fun to join the wolves in the pub. Howl at the moon, all that jazz. Or maybe there's someplace nearby that has dancing. Remember how we used to always go dancing? How it relieved all of our problems?"

Before we became blood mates, when I was severely depressed, Jareth took me out to Club Fang, promising me that a night of music and dance would be just the ticket to cheer me up. And he was right, too. There's something about the power of dance that lifts a bad mood. If only I can get him to agree to go.

But he only shakes his head. "Sorry, Rayne," he says. "I think our problems are a little more serious than the kind that can be cured by a song and dance."

They are? Since when? This is getting a bit worrisome.

"Why are you so down, Jareth?" I ask, walking over to him, searching his face for answers. "I mean, we're going to accomplish our mission. Save the day once again. You should be happy."

He stares back at me blankly and I can't tell what he's thinking at all. Geez. Back in America I couldn't get him to stop smiling for five seconds. Yet now that *I'm* happy, he's total Emo boy again. Why can't we just get mood-synced for once?

I put my arms around his waist, trying to pull him close. But his body is stiff and unyielding. He grabs my hands and pulls them away, then pushes by me and walks over to the bed and sits down.

"Jareth, what's wrong?" I ask, a scared tickle creeping through my insides. I shiver, hugging my arms to my chest. The room's suddenly as cold as Christmas and I have the horrible feeling there's no Santa Claus on his way.

Jareth draws in a deep breath, folding his hands in his lap. "Rayne, we need to talk," he says at last. His voice sounds a bit hoarse.

I freeze. A talk? *A talk?* But that's relationship code for . . .

Oh my God. He's going to break up with me.

I lean against the wall and slump down to a sitting position, hugging my knees to my chest, fighting off the panicky feeling inside—the icy electricity thrumming through my veins, my heart pounding like mad against my chest.

I've finally done it. I've managed to scare him off. My boyfriend. My blood mate. The one who promised to live with me for all time. Problem is, when he made that promise he had no idea what living with me would actually be like. Stupid, pig-headed, angry-at-the-world me.

"Please don't leave me," I whisper. It's an effort to even speak, what with the apple-sized lump in my throat and all. "I love you."

He bows his head, placing it in his hands, and then scrubs his face. When he looks up I realize he may be holding back tears of his own. "I'm sorry, Rayne," he says. "But I just can't do this anymore."

"But we're . . . we're blood mates. We're bound together for eternity!" I protest, not willing to give in without a fight. "You can't just leave me. It's . . . it's like in my contract, right?"

"Contracts can be voided. Of course I'll make sure you have everything you need to live out your days in comfort.

The coven does have strict rules about blood mate alimony and of course I will adhere to them."

My stomach twists in knots. I feel like I'm going to be sick. He's really doing it. Really and truly breaking up with me. "Jareth, please!" I beg. "Don't leave me. I want to be with you. Forever."

"Do you?" He suddenly looks over at me, his eyes sharp and piercing. "Because I don't get that vibe from you."

I swallow hard. "Uh, what do you mean?" I ask, wanting, yet not wanting to hear all the details of why I suck.

"Oh, I don't know," Jareth retorts. "Maybe it's because when I'm nice to you you're a total bitch back to me. When I worry about you, you accuse me of smothering you. When I'm happy and having fun you get annoyed. You're only sweet to me when you want something or it suits your mood."

I stare at my feet, wanting to protest, wanting to defend myself, but having no idea how to do it. Because, I realize, every last thing he says is true. Why would he want me as a blood mate? I don't think I'd want myself.

"Look," he continues. "I just don't think this is going to work out. We gave it the old college try, but it's not happening. When we get back from England I'll petition the council to release us from our bounds."

"But . . . but . . ." But I can't come up with any more arguments.

"Don't worry, Rayne," Jareth says, his voice softening. "They won't cast you out. They'll try to set you up with a new blood mate. One you'll be more compatible with."

"But I don't want a new blood mate," I sob. "Please, Jareth. I don't want to lose you."

"Don't you get it, Rayne?" he asks, tears in his beautiful green eyes. "You already have."

20

I feel like I've been crying for days. Curled up in the king-sized, four-poster bed at Appleby Manor, sobbing hysterically, barely able to breathe. Jareth took off soon after he made his pronouncement, saying he would be staying in another room tonight and would meet me to pick up the antidote tomorrow morning. I begged him to stay, made a complete fool of myself with my groveling, but it did no good.

Night falls and I realize I'm starving. I consider room service, but then decide that it might be best to leave the hotel room. Maybe I'll find Jareth in a local pub or something. Then I can talk to him again. Maybe he just needed some time alone. Maybe he'll forgive me.

Yeah, right, Rayne. Keep dreaming.

I choose a simple black dress from the wardrobe and pull it over my head. Then I slip on some black tights and a pair of boots. I don't bother with makeup and just throw my hair up in a ponytail. There's no one I want to impress here and, besides, there's nothing I can do about my puffy, tear-stained face and red eyes.

I lock the hotel room door behind me and head down to the lobby. I ask the concierge if he can recommend a place to eat. Somewhere that serves burgers extra rare. He suggests several pubs, including the one the wolves hang out at. But I want to avoid that place—don't want them to see me in my current state.

As I'm walking to the second pub the concierge mentioned, I pass a cyber café. I decide to go in and write a couple e-mails. E-mails to other people I've pissed off for no reason this past week. Maybe if I preempt them with an apology they won't write me off for life like Jareth has.

So I pay for an hour's worth of computer time, order tea, and sit down at one of the terminals.

Dear Cait:

I know you probably hate me and I can completely understand why. I'm really sorry for what I did and promise you I only had the best intentions—not that that excuses anything.

Anyway, I hope you are seeing a doctor for what we talked about before Mandy walked in. Whether you believe me or not, I really care about you and don't want to see you hurting yourself. I beg you, Cait, just go to the school counselor and ask them what you should do. I'm sure they can help.

I'll be back in a few days. If you can find it in your heart to forgive me, I'll help you in any way I can.

Love,
Rayne

I press send and then continue on to e-mail number two.

Dear Mom:

I'm sorry I blew up and pushed David. That was really uncalled for and I don't know why I did it. I'm going through something hard right now, I think, but it's not fair for me to take it out on you and David. I'm glad you found yourself a guy that you love and I hope it works out between you two.

I'll be home from Spider's as soon as we're done with our big school project. Probably tomorrow night. And I promise I'll be a better daughter when I get back. And I'm going to go see someone about my anger issues.

I love you,
Rayne

I also write an apology letter to David. Then I write an update to Sunny (the one person I haven't pissed off!) about the Lycan antidote and my clever cover story to Mom. I don't mention my breakup with Jareth. Some things are too painful to type into an e-mail.

After sending all the e-mails, I leave the cyber café and head to the pub for some food. I walk inside, saddle up to the bar, and start by ordering a pint of Bass. Might as well dull my sorrows with some alcohol. To my surprise, they don't even ask for my fake ID. Unfortunately, the beer itself is lukewarm and when I question the efficiency of their refrigeration, the bartender laughs and says something that sounds a lot like, "Dumb Yank," under his breath.

"It's a custom in England to drink one's ale at room temperature," says an English-accented male voice next to me. I turn to see a teen around my age sitting down next to me.

"That seems like a lousy custom," I say.

"I always thought so myself," the boy agrees. "Bartender, get us two Coronas." He smiles at me. "Not very English, but at least they serve them cold."

"Cool. Thanks," I say, taking a closer look at my bar buddy and realizing he's extremely cute and totally Goth. He's got long black hair, piercing blue eyes rimmed with eyeliner, and a delicate face with high cheekbones. He's long and lean and dressed all in black, down to the polish on his fingernails.

Great. I finally meet someone in England who won't think I'm a freak and I haven't made any effort to dress cool.

"I've not seen you around," he says, as the bartender hands us our drinks.

"I'm just visiting," I confess. "I'm from America."

"Ah, America. I've not had the pleasure of seeing your fine country for me'self," he says. "Though I've always thought it'd be a fantastic place to holiday. Go to Hollywood, see all the cinema stars."

I laugh. "Well, I live on the opposite end of America," I say. "Like three thousand miles away from any movie stars."

"I'm Orpheus," the boy says, holding out his hand. Wow, what a cool name. I guess I should expect that. Someone so beautiful could not ever have a normal name like Chris or Mike.

"I'm Rayne," I say, placing my hand in his. But instead of shaking it, he brings it to his lips and kisses the back of my palm softly. Just like knights in shining armor used to do. How cool is that?

"It is a pleasure to meet you, Rayne," he murmurs, not letting go of my hand.

I smile, feeling my face heat a bit. What am I doing? Sure this guy is hot and all, but I've been single for all of five minutes. The last thing I need is to start hooking up with someone random. Not when my heart still belongs to Jareth . . .

I scan the bar, looking for my ex. He's nowhere to be seen. Too bad. Maybe I could have at least made him jealous. Made him realize that though we have our problems, the last thing he wants is for me to start hanging out with someone else.

"So what are you up to this fine evening?" Orpheus asks.

I shrug. "You're looking at it."

"Surely not. You're all dressed up. You definitely need a place to go."

"I'm not really in the mood for partying tonight, actually," I say with a deep sigh. "To tell you the truth, I just broke up with my boyfriend."

"I'm sorry," Orpheus says in a sympathetic voice. "Though that's all the more reason to go out. To forget your worries and sadness. To have a good time and show the bastard you don't need him."

I think about it for a moment. Maybe he's right. Why mope around in a hotel room when I'm on holiday in England? This is a once in a lifetime opportunity. Do I really want Jareth to ruin it for me?

"What did you have in mind?" I ask.

"There's a rave out in the woods tonight," he says. "If you're into that sort of thing."

Ooh, a rave. A real, English rave. Am I into that sort of thing? I am, I am.

"Where is it?"

"I can take you, if you like. It's in the woods, not far from here."

Here's the point where common sense stands up and waves his little red flags in front of my face, reminding me that the guy's a complete stranger and I'm about to head out into the woods alone with him. *What if he's an axe murderer?* common sense demands. *What if he wants to chop you up into little bits and feed them to his pigs?*

My common sense can be way overdramatic. Which is why I barely ever listen to it. Instead, I remind it that I am a vampire, and thus immortal. The axe may tickle a bit, but it won't render me helpless. And he really doesn't look like a pig farmer to me. So unless the guy's got a wooden stake in his pocket (or is he just happy to see me?) I'm totally safe.

Unless this guy is actually Lone Wolf. The one who infected all the cheerleaders . . .

But no, that's stupid, I remind myself. Shantel said that guy was a total jock. Blond and beefy and Brad Pittesque.

This guy is dark and thin and looks much more like Ville from HIM than Brad. There's no way it's the same person.

"Okay. Sounds like a plan."

I wonder for a moment if I should tell Jareth where I'm going. But I have no idea where he is or how to reach him. Not to mention he'll probably get all pissy if I tell him I'm going to a rave in the middle of the woods. He's worse than my common sense when it comes to things like that.

The bartender comes over to drop off the bill. Orpheus plunks down a couple of brightly colored English bills and tells the guy to keep the change before I can even reach in my purse. Nice.

"If some surfer dude with a dumb Batman shirt comes looking for me," I tell the bartender, "just say me and my new friend Orpheus went to a rave. Tell him I'll be back by morning." There, that ought to cover me. By the time he starts looking I'll already be back.

"Ready?" I ask Orpheus. He nods. "Then let's go dancing."

We're only out in the woods about ten minutes before I can feel the bass deep in my bones. A few minutes later I start seeing flashing lights through the trees. I smile. Orpheus wasn't lying. There is a rave. And it sounds like it's hopping. I'm about to have a very good night. I'm going to dance and party and not think about Jareth for one second. Starting now.

We step into the clearing. There are probably two hundred kids here, all gyrating to a hard techno beat. A makeshift tent in one corner houses the DJ booth, and a large dreadlocked man wearing headphones on one ear masterfully spins the tunes. They've got generators set up to run the flashing, multicolored lights and there's even a refreshment stand serving water and juice.

"Wow!" I say, though of course my voice is completely drowned out by the music. "This is amazing."

Orpheus grabs my hand and drags me into the center of the action. We're soon enveloped in a pool of sweaty people— black, white, Indian, Asian, fat, athletic, Nicole Richie–thin. All together, dancing as if there's no tomorrow, no world outside this circle. It's as if they're one mind, one body, all serving a common purpose. All worshipping the techno beat. I'm totally digging the vibe already and I start dancing, determined to have a good time.

Orpheus beckons one of the dancers over and they talk in each other's ears for a moment. I can't hear what they're saying over the music, but watch as Orpheus gives the kid a wad of bills and the kid slips something in my new friend's palm. Hmm. I'm pretty sure I know what's going on here.

Sure enough, Orpheus turns back to me, smiling, and instructs me to open my mouth. I shake my head. One, I'm not really the druggie kind of girl. I'm mean, sure I've experimented, but only in safe, controlled environments, surrounded by friends.

His face falls and then he offers again.

"Come on," he says. "It'll help you forget your troubles and just enjoy the night."

I hedge. I mean, technically I am a vampire. I'm immortal. The drugs won't hurt me. And it *would* be nice to just leave everything behind and float away in a drug-induced haze. All I've done lately is work. I mean, why did I become a vampire in the first place if I intended on living life the same way I always have?

But all the justification in the world won't reconcile that years of "just say no" that were beaten into me through televised PSAs as a child. And logic keeps reminding me that I'm out in the middle of the woods with a stranger. The last thing I need to do is lose my head.

"No thanks. I'm good," I tell him, though I'm sorely tempted to just say yes. "Let's just dance, okay?"

He looks annoyed, but stuffs the pills in his pocket and wraps his hands around my waist. His touch is electric and soon I'm lost in the dance, the music tickling my earlobes and the flashing, colored lights seducing my eyes in a spell more powerful than any drug. For the first time in months I just feel good. Right. Enjoying the moment instead of stressing over every little thing. All my problems seem a million miles away. I'm here. Now. Happy. Forever.

Well, maybe not forever. But for now. And that's good enough.

Orpheus pulls me closer. We grind against each other, giggling as we gyrate to the beat. He's so sexy. So cool. I'm totally in lust. I try to summon up a guilty feeling for Jareth, who's probably sitting alone in his hotel room, watching infomercials or something, but the music prohibits any feelings of remorse. And in any case, what do I care what he thinks? He broke up with me. His choice. So screw him.

We dance for hours, sucking down bottle after bottle of water. (Even vamps need hydration.) I meet several other ravers who hug me and welcome me and offer me lollypops and small toys and stickers. I feel like I'm part of some happy family that's invited me into their home with open arms. No one judges me here. For how I look, how I act, where I come from. They simply accept me into their hazy, drug-induced circle.

Finally Orpheus takes my hand and drags me away from the crowd.

"I need a break!" he says, laughing. "You're unstoppable."

We walk over to a raging bonfire at the corner of the clearing and sit down on the ground near it. I hold my hands up to feel its warmth. Orpheus gets behind me and starts rubbing my back. "Mmm, that feels good," I purr. "Don't stop."

"Stop rubbing the shoulders of a beautiful girl? Not bloody likely," he says.

I notice the darkness is lifting. The sky lightening to a bruised purple. It's got to be almost dawn. I look at my *Nightmare Before Christmas* watch. Four A.M.

"I've got to get back," I say, though the idea of walking anywhere sounds like such an effort at this point. The dance-fueled adrenaline is fading, draining from my system, sweating out my pores, and I'm suddenly feeling really gross. My skin feels clammy. My head hurts. My stomach is sick. And mentally I've gone from sky high, to rock-bottom low.

What comes up, must come down.

What was I thinking? How could I have just taken off with a stranger, not telling anyone where I was going? What if Jareth came back to my hotel room? What if he wants to offer me an apology, say he wants to get back together, and then he realizes I'm gone? What if I missed my one chance for reconciliation?

I'm so stupid. So, so stupid.

"Don't go!" Orpheus begs. He stops rubbing my back and scrambles around to face me. He takes my hand in his and brings it to his lips once again, looking up at me with sad eyes. "I've had a lovely night. I don't want to lose you at the break of dawn."

I smile a little. He's sweet. Very Emo. Totally my type. If my heart didn't belong to Jareth, that is. But it does, I realize. And no matter what it takes, no matter how long, I have to get him back.

"Sorry," I say. "I have to. I've got things to do, people to see." Ex-boyfriends to reconcile with . . .

"But my love, what could be more important than us being together?" Orpheus asks.

Uh . . . I stare at him. That came out a bit creepy sounding. But maybe he's just overdramatic.

"Sorry, dude," I say with a shrug. "It's been fun. And I'll never forget my first English rave. But I've got to go. I'm heading back to America this afternoon."

"I understand," Orpheus says, reaching over and pressing a cool hand against my hot cheek. I freeze as he lightly caresses my skin, wondering how to back away gracefully. But before I can manage to do so, the boy leans forward and presses his lips against mine.

Panic slams my insides. I can't do this. I don't want to do this. I don't care if Orpheus is totally Goth and hot. All I want is Jareth. Forever and always. Even if he wants to be a surfer dude for the rest of his life.

I gently push Orpheus away. "No," I say. "I can't. I'm sorry."

He frowns, sticking his lower lip out into a pout. "Why not?"

"I'm . . . well, I'm with someone. Sort of."

"I thought you said you'd broken up," he growls, his face darkening.

Argh. Now he's going to think I'm a total tease. Which I am, I guess. I should have never let this get so far. "We did," I say. "But I'm not sure it's for good. I really still love him. Being out here tonight made me realize that. Don't get me wrong—you're great. Totally hot and a lot of fun. But I'm just not . . . well, I'm not over Jareth."

"I see," Orpheus says, his voice ice-cold. "Well, I am sorry to hear that."

"I'm sorry. I really am. I feel bad if I led you on in any way."

"I'll take you back to Appleby," he says stiffly, rising to his feet. "Follow me."

Thank goodness. He's taking this better than I thought he might. Last thing I need is for him to go all psycho on me. Especially when I'm feeling like such crap and have no idea where I am.

So we head back out into the woods, down a narrow trail, and around a bend. I'm glad I have a guide—the landscape looks totally different in the daylight and I'd probably get forever lost in these twisty woods.

We walk and walk. For some reason it seems to be taking a lot longer to get back than I remember it taking to get there in the first place. And I really don't remember going up a steep hill . . .

"Uh, Orpheus?" I question as the woods fall away and I realize we're climbing up what appears to be some sort of mountain. The wind whips through my hair and suddenly I'm freezing cold. I should have worn a jacket at least. "Where are we going? This isn't the way back to Appleby, is it?"

"Shortcut," he explains.

Hmm. "Shortcut?" I repeat. "Up a mountain?"

"Well, long cut, actually," he confesses. "I wanted to show you something before we go back."

Argh. How annoying. The last thing I want right now is a guided tour of jolly old England. My body is aching and my head is pounding. All I want to do is crash in my warm, soft hotel bed. To find Jareth and apologize and beg him to reconsider his decision to leave me.

"No offense, Orph. I'm sure what you want to show me is way cool and all, but actually, I'm beat," I attempt. "Maybe I could come see it another time." Or, like, never. Never would be good.

"It's just a few more yards away," Orpheus says. "Then we can head back to Appleby. I promise it's worth it."

"Fine." I trudge a little higher. I mean, what choice do I have? I've not a clue where I am and so I'm dependent on him leading me back. Why, oh, why did I put myself in this situation to begin with?

"Here we are!" Orpheus calls down, way ahead of me at this point. Thank God, I don't have to walk anymore. I may be a vampire, but that doesn't give me the lung capacity of a killer whale by any stretch of the imagination. Especially after a night of dancing.

I walk up to where he's standing and see we've come to a small ledge that leads into a cave, cut into the hillside. I peer in. It's bigger on the inside than I imagined it to be. I can't even see the back wall. I take a step in, checking out the cave paintings on the wall. The overwhelming theme is dogs hunting stuff. Weird. Though I guess I should be grateful they aren't playing poker. I wonder if this place once housed cavemen or something. Though the paintings don't really look that old. And I doubt they had fluorescent orange paint back in prehistoric days.

"What is this place?" I ask.

"It's where I live," Orpheus says with a smile. "Do you like it?"

Huh? I turn to look at him, confused. "Where you live? You're joking, right? I mean, you can't live here."

"Why not? The cave has everything I need." He twirls around, hands out to accentuate the *everything*, which from my vantage point is not much more than four walls, tacky artwork, and a mound of dirt. "Shelter, a nearby stream, protection. It's perfect."

Wow, I had no idea the guy I'd partied with was a Goth Grizzly Adams. Very, uh, weird.

"All it needs is a family," Orpheus adds, sounding a bit wistful.

I stare at him, suddenly getting that creepy feeling inside again. "I'd like to go home now," I say, putting my foot down. "Please show me the way."

Orpheus shakes his head. "I'm afraid that's impossible."

Fear strikes through my heart. "What? Why?" Oh my God, oh my God. What have I gotten myself into now?

"Because, my darling," he says with a twisted smile. "You are the chosen one. The alpha female worthy to become my mate."

21

"Your *what?*" I cry, horrified, disgusted, and freaked out beyond belief. "What the hell are you talking about, dude?"

But it's really a rhetorical question at this point. The cave, the mate thing, the dog paintings. I'm adding up two plus two here and even math-challenged me ain't getting five.

I try to back out of the cave, but Orpheus blocks my exit, moving faster than my eyes can follow. It's then that I notice the tufts of hair peeking from his sleeves. His black painted fingernails lengthening into claws.

"You're Lone Wolf," I whisper. "The renegade Lycan who infected the Oakridge High cheerleaders. I thought you were a jock."

He rolls his eyes. "I'm a shape-shifter. I can take on any human form I choose." He smiles smugly, all while his face elongates before my very eyes. Whiskers sprout from his previously clean-shaven skin. Fangs protrude from his mouth. Eyes narrow and brighten to a brilliant yellow. I can't believe he's shape-shifting right here, right now. I watch, too fascinated and horrified to turn away.

"I left the Order a few months ago," Orpheus explains. "I was sick to death of taking orders from that bastard wolf Lupine. I felt it would be best to start my own pack. Find myself some bitches and start mating. I will be the grand sire of this new, elite pack. And have many wolves under my command."

"Dude, I've heard of some crazy ways to pick up chicks in my day, but let me tell you, I think in this day and age most of us would prefer—"

"Silence!" he growls. "You will speak when spoken to, female."

I bolt toward the cave entrance, but again, he's too fast. This time he grabs me by the shoulders and pins me against the cave wall. I cry out in pain as my back slams against solid rock. Orpheus's face is inches from mine and he's ninety percent wolf now, though still standing on his hind legs and wearing clothing. He growls at me, saliva dripping down his fanged mouth. I start to scream for help.

He laughs, but it sounds more like a howl. "Yell all you want," he says. "We're far away from any towns."

I close my mouth. He's right, of course. Right now I might as well be in outer space. Either way, no one can hear me scream.

"What do you want from me?" I demand, trying to keep up the tough-girl act. Isn't that what you're supposed to do with snarling dogs? Show them you're not afraid, even if you very, very much are afraid?

"I told you," he says, claws digging into my shoulders, "I want you as my alpha bitch. The other American girls I turned, they proved . . . not worthy. Not like you. You're so fair. So . . ." He leans his nose into my neck and breathes in. ". . . so smelly."

Smelly? Uh, right. Damn, I forgot to suppress my vampire scent before I went out. Stupid, Rayne, really stupid.

"Look, man—er, wolf," I say. "You're barking up the wrong skirt, here. I'm a vampire. I can't exactly become a werewolf, too."

"I don't believe you. If you were a vampire you could easily overtake me. Everyone knows vampires are much more powerful than us dogs."

"Well, I . . . I . . ." Sigh. Did I mention how much it sucks to be a gimped vampire with no powers? And why, oh why, didn't I pack a pistol full of silver bullets before I left the hotel this evening? "I might overpower you at any second!" I bluff. "So you'd better let me go now while there's still a chance I'll take it easy on you."

It's then that I remember I do have one vampire power. I can send telepathic cries for help to other vampires. Maybe if I send strongly enough Jareth will be able to hear me. Hopefully he's not too mad at me to not at least come to my rescue.

I reach inside myself and pull together as much power and energy as possible, then send out the loudest mental scream for help I can muster. I'm not exactly sure what to say, but I give as much info as I can. Hopefully it will be enough for him to find me.

While I'm yelling my head off on the inside, Orpheus proceeds to tie me up on the outside, binding my hands and feet with a length of rope. Then he sits me down in front of the cave and gathers wood for a fire. "I've killed us a nice rabbit, my darling," he says, after sparking the blaze. He reaches into a wooden box and pulls out the most foul, rotting creature I've ever seen. "I'll roast it for us." He stokes the fire, only managing to produce more smoke. I cough in protest. But that's nothing to what I'm going to feel when he force-feeds me last week's Thumper.

I try to send out another cry for help—I mean, what else can I do? This time I describe Orpheus, too. Maybe Jareth can ask the other Lycans about him. Maybe they know where his cave is so he can come rescue me before it's too late. Before Lycan turns me into a werewolf and tries to (ew!) mate me.

One thing's for sure. I'm so not rolling over and playing dead to this dog.

22

After our "dinner" of roast Thumper, which, of course, I puke right up after being forced to eat, Orpheus tells me he has things to do, dogs to see, and that he'll be back in a few hours. He leaves me tied up just outside the cave.

It's cold, it's damp, and my butt is frozen on the stone ground. Add that to the fact that I'm freaking out scared and you get a pretty good idea of the situation. I'm stuck by a northern English cave on the side of a mountain, miles from any town or village. I've been kidnapped by a werewolf who wants to make me the queen, er, bitch of his pack. And no one has any idea where I am.

Why, oh why, did I think it was a good move to leave the safety of the village and go off with some random guy? Why didn't I at least tell someone where I was going? And why isn't Jareth answering my calls? I've been sending for what seems like hours now and still there's no sign of him. Maybe he doesn't care about me anymore. After all, me being gone kind of eliminates the need of having to annul the blood mate thing. Maybe my cry for help was the best news he heard all day.

Jareth. Tears drip from my eyes as I think about him. The wonderful, most perfect, sweet, kind blood mate a vampire girl could ever hope for. I had him. He loved me. And what did I do? I went and ruined everything. As usual. God, I'm so stupid. Why can't I ever see how good I have it until it's too late? I could have been with him for eternity. Now I'm likely to spend the rest of my (possibly very short) life as part dog. Not that I don't deserve that and a lot more for the way I acted. I wonder if he'll ever be able to forgive me. If I ever see him again, that is.

Will he still take the antidote back home to America? Will he figure out a way to administer it to the cheerleaders? Or will Slayer Inc. step in and decide to euthanize them after all since I'm not there to fight it? And what about Cait? Will they just assume she's one of the wolves and kill her, too, for no reason?

That's it. I have to get out of here. Some way, somehow. Whatever it takes. I can do this. I mean, I'm a vampire. And a slayer. You'd think I'd have some secret weapon at my disposal to getting myself out of this mess. Any moment now I'll think of what that is . . .

"Mmmmhmm."

I freeze. What's that sound? It's coming from the cave. Are there more people here, too? Other captives? Or more wolves? Should I make my presence known or be as quiet as possible? I squint, trying to see inside, but all I can see is blackness.

"Help! Someone help us!" the voice begs.

"Trevor, shut the eff up, dude. I'm telling you, no one can hear you except that psycho wolf guy. And I really don't want him coming back in here and screwing with us again, do you?"

My mouth drops open. I'd know that voice anywhere.

"Mike?" I cry. "Mike Stevens?"

Silence, then, "Who wants to know?"

"Mike? Trevor? It's me. Rayne McDonald."

"What the . . . ?" Mike starts, then he swears under his breath. "Great. I must be hallucinating again. I thought I just heard that freak girl Rayne from school calling out my name."

I frown. Freak girl. Forget the homecoming game. I should really leave those two for wolf meat.

"Nah, dude. I heard her, too," Trevor says. "Unless we're both imagining it. Wouldn't that be way freaky? If we went insane together and, like, saw the same hallucinations and crap?"

I roll my eyes. Tweedledee and Tweedledum are going to be such great pack mates. "You're not hallucinating," I inform them. "I'm here. Just outside the cave." I squint again and think maybe I can make out two dark shapes by the far wall.

"Really? What are you doing here? How did you find us? Did you bring help? That wolf guy is really strong."

"It's a long story. And no, I don't have help. I'm stuck here, too. Well, I'm hoping my backup will show, but I'm not sure that's going to happen. We may have to figure a way out ourselves."

"Yeah, good luck with that."

"How did you guys get here?" I ask, still shocked at their sudden presence. "I mean, we aren't exactly in Massachusetts anymore."

"We don't really know," confesses Mike. "One minute I've just won a football game and the next morning I'm on a plane to England. It's like something . . . or someone . . . was pulling me to this spot. I couldn't eat or sleep until I got here. It was the craziest thing ever."

"Yeah, I only got here a few days ago," adds Trevor. "But same story. Freaking bizarre."

"I've been here over a month now. And I haven't figured out any way to escape," Mike says. He pauses, then adds,

"What does he want from us, Rayne?" His voice cracks. "I'm starting to think we're going to die here."

It's strange to hear him sound so vulnerable. The big, tough football player. The meanest guy in school. I guess being trapped in a cave on the side of a mountain in the middle-of-nowhere England for a month can do that to a guy. Maybe at the very least he's learned some life lessons and will be a kinder, gentler Mike Stevens when/if we get out of this mess.

"Okay, I'll tell you, but you probably won't believe me," I say. "You're here because you've been bitten by a Lycan—that's like a werewolf to you and me."

"No shit, Sherlock. We've seen the dude."

"Not him. The cheerleaders. Back home in Oakridge."

The boys are silent for a second. Then Mike says, "Come on, Rayne. We're serious. Don't give us some fairy tale."

"I *am* serious. Remember the girls came to England for cheering competition this past summer?"

"How could I forget," Trevor groans. "I had to go without sex for seven days and seven nights when my baby Shantel went away."

Mike snorts. "Oh whatever. You totally hooked up with Candi that night at—"

"Shut the hell up, man," Trevor hisses. "This chick knows Shantel."

"Uh, uh. There's no way *she* hangs with Shantel."

"They're both on the cheerleading team!"

"What? No freaking way, man. Not Rayne McDonald. She'd never be a cheerleader."

"Dude, she is. I swear it."

I clear my throat. "Uh, boys? Can we try to focus here? You know, trapped in a cave, by an evil, fuzzy werewolf trying to make us part of his sick little pack? You can debate my cheering status and the likelihood of me telling Shantel about this Candi chick once we get out of here."

"Sorry," they mutter in sync.

"But I didn't cheat on Shantel," adds Trevor. "Candi totally jumped me at this party, even after I said—"

"Uh, we were focusing, remember?" I sigh. "So now what we have to do is—"

But I can't finish my sentence because the big bad wolf is back.

Orpheus storms up the hillside and grabs me by the throat, pulling me to my feet. I cough as he crushes my larynx, making it nearly impossible to breathe.

"You told the Order," he growls. "You told them about my American pack. My she-wolves across the sea." He drops me and I fall back to the ground, slamming my butt against the stone.

"Yes, I did," I say, trying to sound braver than I feel. "And the Order is currently mixing up an antidote for all of them. Your pack of wolf bitches will soon transform back into a squad of human—well, some may still refer to them as bitches. And as for you—"

I stagger sideways as Orpheus cuffs me upside the head.

"How dare you interfere!" he says, slumping down to all fours. "You've ruined everything!"

"For you, maybe. How about them? Do you think they like sprouting fur and fangs every time there's a full moon? I mean, do you have any idea how much laser hair removal and cosmetic dentistry costs these days?"

Orpheus sighs. He blinks a few times, then slides back into human form. It really is a fascinating transformation and I find myself watching closely, briefly wishing I had a video camera to record it and throw it up on YouTube for all to see.

"All I wanted was a pack to call my own," he mumbles, head in his hands. "The Order was so dismissive of me. I never fit in there. I wanted to create a new line of Lycans who would be, would be . . . my friends."

I stare at him. Is he crying?

Suddenly I feel a pang of empathy for the guy. I know more than anyone what it's like not to fit in. For everyone to think you're a crazy freak and not want to be your friend. But still . . .

"You can't force people to become your friends by infecting them with a virus," I reason. "People have to want to be your friends."

"No one ever wanted to be my friend."

I can't believe I'm feeling pity for the guy who's kidnapped me and tied me up. "Look, I understand what you're going through. I'm an outcast of sorts as well. I don't fit in with anyone at school. And none of the vampires like me either. But you know what? I'm going to have to be okay with that. And not be so angry and hateful all the time. Take my old best friend, Mandy."

"*She* was friends with Mandy?" I hear Mike whisper to Trevor. I'd forgotten for a moment we had an audience.

"See, dude, I told you she was a cheerleader."

"Funny thing about Mandy," I say, ignoring the peanut gallery, "I thought for years that she had ditched me to become one of the popular kids. That she didn't think I was cool enough to hang out with her. But I found out this week that it may have been me who ditched her. Because I was afraid she was leaving me behind, I started rebelling in the other direction. Scorning everything she wanted to become because I was afraid I couldn't become it myself."

"I was always the weakest," Orpheus confesses. "I couldn't run as fast. I couldn't catch any game. None of the female wolves liked me. So I decided to leave and start my own pack. Show them that I didn't need anyone."

"One thing I've learned, Orpheus, is that we can't be afraid to need people in life. I know it makes us seem helpless and weak, but sometimes, admitting you need help can be strong in and of itself." Wow, that sounded pretty good.

Especially since I made it up on the fly. Maybe instead of see-ing a shrink, I should become one.

Orpheus rises to his feet. "You seem like a smart girl, Rayne," he says, sounding apologetic. "I'm really sorry I'm going to have to kill you."

Kill me? Fear shoots through my heart. "Why would you have to kill me?" I cry.

"I have to kill all of you." He shrugs. "The Order knows what I did, thanks to you. Soon they'll find my den and they'll use you as evidence against me. I'll be hanged for my crimes against the pack. And I can't let that happen. So I'll have to kill you and eat the evidence."

Okay, being killed is bad enough. But being eaten as well?

He shape-shifts again, back to wolf form. He slowly ap-proaches me, step by step, paw after paw. Desperate, I flip myself over and attempt to wiggle away like a worm—the most stupid escape attempt known to mankind. My heart pounds in my chest. My body grows numb. Oh my God, I can't believe I'm going to actually die. Die and be eaten by a werewolf. And Jareth will never know what happened to me.

Jareth, please help me! I cry one more time.

A moment later, the wolf is on me, grabbing my leg in his mouth and yanking me backward. Teeth dig into my flesh, piercing my skin as I'm pulled back into the cave. I scream and kick at his face, but he's too strong.

This is it. I'm going to die. But not right away. I'm a vampire and immortal. So I'll be alive for all of it. Every last bite. Until he clamps down on my neck, sharp fangs ripping through sinew, severing my head from my—

Suddenly, out of nowhere, a bat sweeps into view with a high-pitched screech. I look up. It's big, it's black, and heading right toward Orpheus's face. He drops my leg, letting out a bellow of surprise as it attacks, beating its rubbery wings against the wolf's eyes, his nose, his mouth.

I watch, amazed. Could it be? It's impossible. Jareth doesn't have any powers. And the other vampires would never rescue a slayer. Still, I can't imagine this is just some random bat. Somehow or other I've been rescued. The undead cavalry has arrived.

A moment later the bat poofs into a cloud of smoke and suddenly Jareth himself appears on the hillside. I burst into tears, I'm so happy to see him. Big, bad, beautiful Jareth. My true love. My hero. He's dressed all in black, looking gorgeous and powerful. And best of all, he's got a gun in his hand, aimed straight at the wolf. (How he transported that gun while in bat form, I'll never know.)

"No one messes with my Raynie," he states, just before squeezing the trigger.

The gun goes off. The wolf yelps once, then collapses onto the cave floor. It convulses a few times, its chest rising and falling, then goes completely limp.

I stare at the wolf, then up at Jareth, tears of joy now streaming down my face.

He reaches me in an instant, throwing his arms around me and pulling me close. "Oh, Rayne," he murmurs. "I was afraid I'd get here too late."

I bury my face in his shoulder, sobbing and laughing all at the same time. Jareth. My wonderful Jareth. The vamp who saved my life. My blood mate. Forever and always.

"Jareth," I cry. "I'm so glad you came. I was afraid you couldn't hear me."

"Of course I could hear you," Jareth says, leaning down to untie my hands and feet. "I heard you the first time you cried out. It just took me some time to track you down." He rips a piece of his shirt and ties it around my leg to stop the bleeding. Then he helps me to my feet.

I kick Orpheus with my toe, to make sure he's really dead and it's not going to be one of those horror movie scenes where the corpse always rises one more time. But he's total dog meat.

"Silver bullet," Jareth explains. "Just like in the movies."

"I'm so sorry about yesterday," I say, covering his face with kisses. "Well, the last month actually. I've been so stupid. So selfish. You've been wonderful. Everything I could want in a blood mate. And I took it all for granted. I guess I just . . . panicked. I mean, I felt trapped in a way. Like, I couldn't believe I'd be with someone forever. But then, when

I realized I'd lost you, I knew I couldn't face forever without you by my side."

He smiles and kisses me back. "I'm sorry, too, Rayne," he says. "I should have been more sensitive to your feelings. You were a new vamp, just learning the ropes of unlife. As your blood mate, I was the one who was supposed to teach you, be there for you. And yet I was so caught up with the idea of being able to walk out in the sun, I neglected my duties. I became angry and impatient when you floundered on your own, knowing deep inside it was all my fault you weren't adjusting properly. I should have been there for you and I'm sorry I wasn't. I hope you can forgive me."

"Of course I do," I say. "As long as you forgive me for being such a bitch. Vampire transformation, new hormones or no, there's no excuse for how bratty I've been. Especially to you, who I love more than anyone, ever." I press my face against his chest, feeding on his warmth. Suddenly something occurs to me. I look up at him. "Jareth? The way you morphed into a bat . . . do you . . . do you somehow have your powers back?"

Jareth blushes. "Uh," he says. "About that."

"You do!" I exclaim. "How did you get your powers back? And when?"

He shrugs. "I've actually had them back for a few months now. Remember when I opened the locker-room door you couldn't and tried to brush it off like it was no big deal? One day I woke up and realized I'd returned to my former self. Well, I can still go out in the sun, but I'm okay otherwise. I can do everything I used to. I'm not sure why or how, but there it is."

"But that's so great! Why didn't you tell me?"

He hangs his head. "I felt bad. You were all 'we're power-less vamps together' and I didn't want to disappoint you. I kept hoping you'd develop some powers, too, but maybe because you already had the blood virus when I bit you . . . I don't know."

"Jareth, I can't believe you were afraid to tell me! I'm so happy you got your powers back. That's awesome. Maybe you can go be Magnus's general again."

"I'm so glad you're not annoyed, my love."

"No way. I'm thrilled for you. I love you, Jareth. Forever and always. Let's never fight again."

He laughs. "How about we just say let's always make up if we do?" he suggests. "Seems a bit more reasonable a promise to make."

"Hey, Rayne! When you're done with the mushy crap can you get back here and untie us?"

"Yeah. We want to get the hell out of here, too, you know."

Oh yeah. Lost in makeupville, I almost forgotten about Mike and Trevor.

"The missing football players," I explain to Jareth. "They're here. In the cave."

"Excellent," Jareth says, moving to the back of the cave. "It's looking like we might have our happy ending after all."

I smile to myself and hug my arms across my chest. Happily ever after. I like the sound of that.

But first we have some cheerleader wolves to vaccinate.

23

We untie Mike and Trevor, who are obviously still a bit shell-shocked, and head back to Appleby. We bring the boys to Lupine and he checks them over for signs of lycanthropy. Sure enough, they've got traces of the virus in their systems. So Lupine sends them into a full-moon simulator shack at the edge of town and once the moon's pull shapeshifts them to their feral forms, they're sprayed with the antidote and are humanized once again.

The wolves drug them and have a courier escort them back to America before they wake up. The boys won't know what happened to them, they tell us, and so it's better that they don't regain consciousness until they're safe in their hometowns. Sure, people will ask them where they've been all this time—after all, their disappearances have garnered a lot of media attention. But in the end, all that really matters is they're back and not dead.

Unfortunately for me, the cheerleaders are already in America and there's no way to ship them all over to England to put them in the full-moon simulator and administer the antidote on site. But I have an idea of how we might get them to go all hairy and so I take the vials of antidote they made for us, thank the wolves, and Jareth and I head back to America. We spend most of the plane ride in each other's arms and let's just say I'm now a member of a certain exclusive club one can only join when one finds herself mile high.

Mom is overjoyed when I walk in the front door. Says she was worried to death about me and begs me never to run away again.

"I'm sorry about David," she says, sitting me down at the kitchen table and handing me a big bowl of some kind of unidentified food stuff. Even starved me isn't about to take a bite of that. "It was selfish of me to have him move in before you two were ready. This is a new experience for all of us and I have to be more considerate of you and your feelings. After all, this is your house, too. And the last thing I want is for you to feel uncomfortable in your own home. I should have talked to you two before making my decision. Especially before kicking you out of your own room. I don't know what I was thinking. We're a family. A democracy." She swallows hard. "If you want me to stop seeing David, I will. You girls are the most important thing in my life and if you're not ready for me to date, I won't date."

I think for a moment. In a way it would be great to have Mom back to ourselves. To get rid of the stranger invading our space. But I take one look at her face and realize I could never do that to her. She loves him. Like I love Jareth. And yet she's willing to sacrifice everything she wants to make us happy. But that's not fair. She's Mom, not some tortured saint. She deserves to have her own happiness. And even if David is kind of a dork, he's her dork. And I'm suddenly okay with that.

"Oh, Mom," I say, trying to sound all business. "David's not that bad, I guess. Could be a lot worse. And he can cook. We need someone in this house with some culinary expertise."

Mom's face lights up like Christmas morning. "So you . . . you don't mind if he stays?"

I shrug nonchalantly. "Yeah, might as well. I'm getting pretty used to sharing a room with Sunny and we wouldn't want the extra bedroom to go to waste."

Mom reaches over and pulls me into a hug. "Oh, Rayne," she whispers in my ear. "Thank you, sweetie. You're the best daughter a mother could ever hope to have."

"Not really," I say, hugging her back. She smells like cinnamon. Like Mom. I'm so glad to be home. "But I'm working on it."

I return to school Monday morning and sneer at all my teachers who give me attitude for missing my classes without a sick pass from the office. I may be working toward a kinder, gentler Rayne, but teachers are so exempt from that status. Unless they want to bribe me with good grades, that is, though sadly I've never gotten any of them to take me up on my oh-so-generous offer.

Cait finds me in the hallway and throws her arms around me in a hug. I step back, surprised. This is not the reaction I was thinking she'd have when we met again. After all, the last time I saw her she was telling me to leave her the eff alone. Here's hoping she isn't carrying any concealed weapons to stab me in the back with.

"Oh, Rayne," she cries. "I've been looking all over for you. I have to thank you!"

"Thank me?" What did I do to deserve thanking? Last I heard, I'd ruined her life.

"For being honest with me. About my, well, you know." She blushes as she steals a glance down at her arms. "I realized you were right. I couldn't go on hurting myself like that. And to tell you the truth, it wasn't really working anymore anyway. It started out making me feel better, but after a while I just felt so guilty and ashamed I ended up feeling worse. And I was so afraid all the time—worried that someone would catch me doing it."

"So did you . . . ?"

"I went to the school counselor. And she told me she could talk to my mom for me. And she promised me she'd be able to do it in a way that my mom wouldn't get mad. At first I didn't believe her, but somehow she did. My mom was really worried, of course, but she never yelled at me once. It turns out she's been suffering from an eating disorder most of her life. She's in recovery now, but she still totally gets where I'm coming from. Over the weekend we found this great therapist who's going to start teaching me what she calls coping mechanisms so I don't feel like hurting myself again. I'm sure it's not going to be easy, but it's worth it."

"That's great, Cait. I'm so happy for you!" I exclaim. "And um, what about the cheerleading thing?" I add, almost afraid to ask and spoil her good mood.

Cait shrugs. "My mom decided it was a good idea for me to drop out. You know, until I get back on my feet. Which surprised me. I mean, it was always her dream for me to become a cheerleader. I never thought she'd let me quit. But she told me my health is way more important to her than a pair of pom-poms." Cait smiles sheepishly. "She's actually pretty cool, now that we're talking again."

I smile. "I'm so glad for you. Did you tell the others?"

"Yeah. And that's the weirdest thing. I mean, I went into it assuming no one would give a care. You know, since I only made the team because you blackmailed them?"

I cringe. "Well . . ."

Cait holds up a hand. "But when I told them I was leaving, they got all upset. Turns out they really like having me on the team. Said it won't be the same without me and whenever I'm ready to come back I should." She grins. "So though you may have helped get me on the team originally, I've managed to do well enough to stay on it."

"I never doubted that for a second," I say. "You're the best cheerleader on the squad by far and everyone knows it."

"Thanks, Rayne," Cait says. "I'm sorry I was mad before. I was just freaked out and scared. But you know what? I think I'm going to be okay."

"You know what, Cait? I think I am, too." I pull her into another hug, happy the troubled girl has found some peace. Happy that I have, too.

"That's what I hate about this school. Too much PDA in the halls. Girl hugging everywhere you look!" I turn to see my sister walking down the hall, backpack slung over one shoulder. She waves hello and approaches Cait and me.

"So you're back, I see," she says.

"And you've managed to talk your way out of my you-know-where prison cell."

"Meh, that was easy. When you're dating the head guy you can pull in a few favors every once in a while."

"Well, thank you for doing so. I'm pleased to say I got the antidote and operation Save the Cheerleaders is in effect."

Cait raises her eyebrows. "Save the cheerleaders?"

"Um, yeah, you know. From turning into . . . what they turned into the other night."

"So you believe me about that?" she asks, sounding surprised. "You don't think I was just hallucinating or something? I mean, they seem so normal now. I figured maybe I was just under a lot of stress or maybe lost too much blood . . ."

"Nope. You were right. And while they might seem normal now, by the next full moon . . . arrrooooo!" I howl. "Unless we stop them."

"How can we do that?"

"Antidote." I grin. "I went to England to get it."

"Wow. That's, um . . . wow." Cait stammers, sounding not quite sure whether she should believe me or not.

"So what's your daring plan?" Sunny asks. "How are we going to trap the wolves to turn them back?"

"Thank you for asking," I say, pleased to discuss my oh-so-clever strategy. "Well, according to the pack I talked to, there are two ways to get an untrained wolf to go feral. One is the full moon, of course. The other is to get them all hot and bothered."

"So, uh, basically you need to either wait 'til the next full moon or figure out a way to get the entire squad turned on at one time?" Cait asks.

"Yup. And I'm not one for waiting." I pull out a magazine cutout from my bag and unfold it. Race Jameson, rock star extraordinaire, grins back at us from the printed page. "Meet my secret weapon."

"You're going to show them a magazine cutout?" Cait exclaims.

"Not exactly," I say, flashing a grin at Sunny. She nods, knowing right where I'm going with this one. "But you'll see soon enough. First, I need to get all the cheerleaders in one place." I turn to Cait. "And that's where you come in."

24

It's seven P.M. and I'm pacing the living room floor of my house, waiting for my mom to leave. She's taking her damn sweet time getting ready for her date with David. I glance over at him. He's looking at his watch, too. He knows timing is everything and for once I'm glad I have him on my side. He may be an annoying future stepfather figure, but he's still an operative of Slayer Inc. and has operation Get Mom Out of the House under control.

"Sweetie, our dinner reservations are in a half hour," he calls up the stairs. "We need to get going."

"Just a minute, David. I'm putting on lipstick."

"Gah, before she met you she didn't own a tube of lipstick," I mutter.

He laughs. "Hey, she looks gorgeous wearing it. I'm not going to fight that battle."

"Yeah, yeah. Tell her to apply it in the car. The cheerleaders will be here any minute now and we can't let Mom know we're staging a save-the-town party in her living room on a school night. She'd absolutely kill me."

"Are you sure everything's in place?" David walks over and rechecks the front door. "Automatic locks working?"

"Yup. I tested them a few minutes ago. You did a great job putting them in." I press a remote control and the entire house seals up. I release the button and it's an open house again.

"Thanks. I used to be an engineer before I joined Slayer Inc. So I'm pretty handy with rigging up this kind of stuff."

"Yeah, well, I . . . appreciate it. I couldn't have set this up without you." It kills me to compliment the guy, but he did put a lot of work into this plan.

"No problem." He grins. "It's all in a day's work."

"Yeah, but I know how you feel about me. And I haven't been very grateful."

"Don't worry. I get it. I'm your guardian and I'm also dating your mom. That must be pretty weird for you."

I shrug. "I don't know."

"Aw, come on, Rayne. Of course it is. Some strange guy comes into your home, kicks you out of your room, spends all his free time with your mom. It's gotta be rough."

"Okay, fine. It is a bit . . . annoying. Especially the room part. Or the mom part. I don't know. It's all weird. Nothing against you personally. Just, we've been an all-girl family for a long time."

"I have to tell you something, Rayne," David says, his voice growing serious. "My condo isn't really being painted."

"What? What do you mean?" I stare at him, once again angry. Was this just his clever ruse to get into Mom's bed? And here I'd been thinking he wasn't such a bad guy after all. "Why the hell are you here then?"

"Slayer Inc. has had reports of a new threat coming into town. We're not sure of the details, but there's been intelligence that it may be after someone in your family. They're keeping it on the down low. I'm not even supposed to know this. But I heard it from a very reliable source. So I decided I should stay close, just in case," he says. "I love your mom, Rayne. And I want to protect her family as best I can."

"Oh my God!" I cry. "Something's coming after our family? But why? 'Cause Sunny's Magnus's girlfriend? Or 'cause I'm the slayer?"

"They don't know. But actually they think it might have something to do with your mother."

"What? But Mom's not a part of any of this! She's an innocent bystander. She doesn't even know the supernatural world exists."

"There's more to your mom than you know, Rayne," David says mysteriously.

"Like what?"

Footsteps start down the stairs. Mom's on her way down. David lowers his voice. "No time to explain. But know this: I'm here living in your house to ensure your mother and you girls are protected. Because I care about all of you. Whatever it is, whenever it comes, I will do everything to keep you all safe."

Suddenly the nerdy house invader looks somewhat like a superhero in the dim lighting.

"Thanks," I whisper back. "Just promise to keep me in the loop. After all, I'm still the slayer, right? Maybe I can even help."

He nods, then straightens to address my mother. "Don't you look gorgeous," he exclaims, whistling.

My mom beams, twirling around. She's wearing a gauzy pink dress with a rose-petal pattern. She does look gorgeous. And happy, too. I remember how bored and sad she used to be before she met David. He's good for her, whether I want to admit it or not. And if he's really here to keep us safe, then that's even better.

"Go! Go!" I urge, remembering the timing we're working under. Future threats must be sent to the back of my mind.

Tonight, I have to catch and cure me some werewolves. "Enjoy dinner. Have a good time. Vacate the premises!"

Mom narrows her eyes. "Why are you so anxious for us to leave, Rayne?" she asks. "Are you planning something?"

"Yeah, to watch the new vampire movie I Netflixed. It's supposed to be fangfully fresh."

"Rayne's fine," David interjects. "But we're late. Let's get a move on."

Of course Mom listens to him and a moment later they're out the door and I can hear their car driving away.

Not five minutes later, the doorbell rings. I rush to answer it. It's Cait, accompanied by Shantel, Nancy, Mandy, and a couple of the other girls. They're dressed for a party and they carry goodies. Shantel's brought a plate of cupcakes and the others have chips, soda, and candy. Too bad I can't eat anything.

"Come on in," I say. "Put the stuff down on the table here. Let me take your coats."

I can't believe I, Rayne McDonald, am playing party hostess for the Oakridge High cheerleading squad. But, hey, when you're saving the world, sometimes you have to break character.

Shantel sets down her cupcakes and turns to me, eyes shining. "You'll never believe it, Rayne," she says. "Trevor's back! And Mike's with him! The two of them just showed up last night, wandering through town. It's the craziest thing. They don't remember where they've been or anything."

"Wow. That's insane," I say, giving her my best innocent surprise look. "But I'm glad they're back before the homecoming game! What would we have done without them?"

The doorbell rings. More guests, armed with goodies. I turn up the music and several people move back the couch to clear the living room for dancing. Others gather around the food and sodas, talking amicably amongst themselves. It's like a real party and everyone's having a good time. Almost a shame it's going to end soon—with raining werewolf antidote.

I notice Mandy standing away from the other girls, as if she feels an outsider to all the action. I consider going over and talking to her, maybe even trying to make some sort of peace between us. But I realize my well-meaning attempts may end with her bolting from the house and thus missing out on her cure.

There'll be time to talk later. To apologize. And I plan to do so.

I glance at my watch, too nervous to enjoy myself. Sunny should be back by now. I hope she didn't run into any trouble picking up our bait.

Then, as if on cue, headlights swing into the driveway. They're here. Operation Save the Cheerleaders can begin. I do a quick head count. Yup, everyone's here.

I turn to the front door. Sunny walks in the house first, a silly grin on her face. She's obviously enjoyed her trip in the car with our special guest. She shuts the door behind her and throws me a nod, indicating everything's ready. I turn down the music and address the crowd.

"Thank you all for coming," I say. "Cait really appreciates everyone coming to her good-bye party."

There's a spattering of applause. Cait blushes.

"But this isn't just your ordinary chips and dips affair," I continue. "Tonight, we have a special surprise for you."

The doorbell rings. I walk over to the door. Everyone's watching.

"Tonight," I say theatrically, "tonight I give you Race Jameson!" I whip open the door and everyone gasps as they lay eyes on the rock star standing behind it.

Race is wearing tight black leather pants and a silk black shirt, halfway unbuttoned down the front. Way too tacky for my taste, but I can hear the oohs and aahs as he flashes the cheerleaders his trademark grin. "Hey, girls," he says saucily. "I'm Race Jameson. And I'm here to light your fires!"

I roll my eyes. Could he be any cheesier? He's a vampire, for goodness sake, didn't he learn any class from the old days? But, whatever, he's not here to read Shakespeare or impress us with his intellect.

He's here to put these wolves in heat.

Race slips a CD in the CD player and soon saucy jazz spills from the speakers. He starts gyrating to the beat, pulling off his shirt slowly, revealing his muscular chest. The girls scream and squeal as they realize what's going on. Their idol, the number-one rock star in the country, is doing a striptease, just for them.

"I can't believe Race agreed to do this," Sunny whispers.

"Actually, he looks like he's enjoying himself."

"Just make sure he doesn't take a bite out of one of the girls. Magnus says he's always hoping to add a pretty face to his harem of blood donors."

I laugh. "Look, Sun, I think it's working!"

We switch our focus from the stripper rock star to his squealing fans. Sure enough, some of them are starting to sprout hair. Just a bit here and there and none of the others have noticed yet. A few tufts billowing from their chests, a few hairs sprouting from their cheeks.

"Oh, Race!" Mandy cries. She's the hairiest of them all at this point. She's even started growing a snout. "You rock my world!"

The others laugh and turn to look at her. Then they freeze.

"Oh my God, Mandy!" cries Shantel. "You're—you're!" She stares at her, horrified. "What a big nose you have!"

Mandy looks back at her, equal horror on her snouty face. "Shantel! What big teeth you have!"

Panic ensues. Girls are running, screaming, freaking out. Each thinking they look normal, but their squad mate has become a monster.

"Now!" I cry to Sunny. My twin hits the remote, effectively locking everyone in the house. I climb up on a chair and put a lighter to the sprinkler system. A moment later the place is raining werewolf antidote, which David installed in the plumbing. There's more shrieking as the girls are doused with the cure. They're running around, trying to escape. But even their werewolf strength can't break David's locks. We should keep the system installed after this whole thing is over. You never know when an airtight house might come in handy.

Luckily the antidote works quickly and moments later everyone's back to their old selves again. No more hair, teeth, claws, or snouts. Just soaking wet cheerleaders, staring at a soaking wet, half-naked Race Jameson. They all look around, completely confused, not remembering how or why they got all wet.

"W00t! Wet T-shirt contest!" Race cries. "And I'm judging!"

It's more than an effective distraction and soon all the girls are strutting their stuff, hoping to impress the rock star in my living room. Well, some things never change.

I cheer, slapping high fives with Cait and Sunny. Once again Rayne McDonald saves the day.

Damn, I'm good.

25

We're down by three, fourth quarter, fourth down, and Mike has the ball. Only seconds to go and the clock on the scoreboard counts down relentlessly. Mike backs up, looks for an opening . . .

We're screaming, we're yelling, we're jumping up and down. "Go, Wolves!" The fans in the packed bleachers echo our cheer. There's a crackling of electricity in the air. A roar from the crowd. It's now or never.

Mike sees Trevor enter the end zone. He's wide open.

As red uniforms converge on our quarterback, Mike throws. Trevor leaps into the air and manages to catch the ball—a split second before he's tackled to the ground.

The Wolves win the homecoming game.

The crowd leaps up in unison, a chaos of blue jackets, hats, and sweaters—cheering and clapping and whooping the old Wolf pack howl.

"Whoo! Yeah! Go Mike and Trevor!" we yell. Mandy does a back flip. Shantel and Nancy jump up and down.

I yell, too, even pulling off a pretty good round-off, coming back up with pom-poms still in place.

Yes, I, Rayne McDonald, am still a Wolves cheerleader. At least for now. After all, I couldn't just abandon my squad simply because I was done with my mission impossible. Homecoming's an important game and I can't have them basket-tossing Nancy without me there to make sure she gets caught.

So I'm a Goth. A vampire. And now a cheerleader. And no one's going to tell me it's not okay to be all three. After all, I've always prided myself as an individual. If I enjoy cheering, then I'll cheer. And if anyone wants to make anything of that, short skirt or not, I'll totally kick their ass across the football field.

Even Mandy admitted, during her pep talk before the game, that I'd come a long way since day one of practice. Now that she's cured, she and I have settled into at least a temporary truce. We may never be best friends again, but at least now we have a grudging respect for one another and both understand a little better where the other is coming from.

"Rayne! Rayne!" My mom's beaming as she runs over to me, waving like a lunatic. Once I finally told her I was a cheerleader she insisted on coming to watch me. Which is pretty cool, I guess. Though slightly embarrassing.

"Hey, Mom," I greet, waving a pom-pom in her direction. She embraces me tightly and I hug her back. My hippie, dippie mom. I love her so much. And like David, I will do anything to protect her.

"Wow, Rayne. You were amazing. Really amazing. I'm so impressed. I had no idea you could do those kinds of moves."

"Well, it did take some practice."

"Yeah, you were really something," David says, walking up behind Mom. "A total natural."

"Isn't she?" Sunny asks, joining the group. "I keep telling her that but she refuses to believe me."

I feel my face heat at all the compliments. I'm so used to being the bad girl. The one everyone's annoyed at or afraid of. It's weird being the center of positive attention. But I guess I can deal with it. At least for tonight.

"Can I speak to you for a minute, Rayne?"

A voice makes me turn around. It's Mr. Teifert. Wow, does everyone and their mother come to these things?

"Well," I say, glancing over at my family. I'm not quite ready for the Rayne adoration to stop.

"We'll be right over here," David assures me, probably figuring Teifert wants to talk Slayer shop. He and Mom and Sunny take a few steps back. I can tell Sunny's trying to keep an ear open though.

"What's up, T?" I ask, wondering if he has another mission for me. Whatever it is, this time I won't argue. Whatever he wants me to do, no matter how crazy it sounds, I'm his girl. I'm Rayne McDonald. I'm the slayer.

"You're no longer the slayer."

I stare at him. "What?" I cry. "What do you mean?"

He smiles. "Bertha's back. She's undergone an extensive diet and exercise rehabilitation program and is now ready to resume her role as slayer. So you're off the hook."

I can't believe it. The girl's been out of commission since she dusted Lucifent and Magnus became coven leader. Been spending time at a fat farm ever since. And now she's back? I know I should be thrilled to hear I'll no longer be required to perform as a slayer, but for some reason I feel disappointed instead.

"So . . . so you don't need me anymore?" I ask, trying to keep a poker face. The last thing I need is for him to see me all upset.

"Nope," Teifert says cheerily. He's probably happy to be rid of me. We never really did bond, what with my bad attitude and all. Bertha's probably way nice to him. "We should be all right without you from now on. Thanks for all your hard work. It's been real, but the beat goes on."

"But . . ." That's it? After all my training and world-saving it's just Adios, Rayne, don't let the door hit you on the way out? That doesn't seem right. And what about David's warning that something evil was on its way? Don't they need me to face it?

"Are you sure you wouldn't like, um, a backup slayer?" I ask. "I mean, David was telling me you guys got some great evil swinging into town sometime soon. What if Bertha's . . . out of practice? Or she needs someone to stand in at dinner-time when there's a big line at the drive-through?"

Teifert sighs. "Let me discuss it with the rest of Slayer Inc. But yes, I think if you want to stay on as a consultant of some sort, it can probably be arranged."

"Thanks!" I grin, not sure why this makes me happy. Maybe I just like knowing I'm needed. "Don't worry, T, I won't let you down. And I'll be totally unobtrusive. You won't even know I'm slaying."

"That's what I'm afraid of." He shakes his head. "I'll be seeing you around, Rayne," he says, then turns and walks toward the parking lot.

I return to where my family's hanging out a few feet away.

"Wasn't that the drama coach?" Mom asks. "What did he want?"

"Nothing much," I bluff. "Tried to convince me I'd make a kick-ass Morgan Le Fay in his King Arthur play. Which I would. But I told him I'm pretty overcommitted at the moment."

"So you're staying on the . . . team?" Sunny asks pointedly. And I realize she doesn't mean as a cheerleader.

"Yeah," I say. "I think so. At least for a bit. Why not, right? After all, they definitely need me."

"Well, congratulations again, Rayne," my mom says, kissing me on the forehead. "I'm really proud of you."

"Yes," David says. "I am as well." And I can tell he means more than my ability to do splits.

"We're going to head home now," Mom says. "It was great to see you perform."

"Thanks, guys!" I say. "Have a good night. I'll catch you later."

Mom and David turn to go. Sunny grins at me.

"A cheerleader," she says. "Who would have thought?"

"Yup. That's me. Multitalented." I grin. "But listen to this. Teifert just tried to get me to quit the slayer thing. I guess Bertha's all recovered and ready to come back. But I told him he should keep me on retainer. After all, he might need me."

"Yeah, especially if what you told me David was saying is true," Sunny says. "You know, about the new danger coming into town."

"Exactly. Bertha's out of practice. And I'm not putting our family in danger just because we have an incompetent, burger-loving slayer on the payroll."

"Well, I know I feel safer knowing you're still on patrol," Sunny assures me. Then she lowers her voice. "By the way," she says, "I've decided to do it."

"Do what?" I ask, feigning complete innocence. As if I don't know exactly what she's talking about. Still, it's amusing to watch her squirm.

"It," she says, her face reddening. "You know, with Magnus."

"Ahhh," I say, realizing what she means. "My little twin is going to lose her innocence once and for all."

Sunny punches me in the shoulder. "Don't put it like that!" she squeals.

"I'm sorry," I say mockingly. "My sister is going to bonk her boyfriend for the first time."

"Rayne! I'm telling you a huge thing! And you—"

I laugh. "I'm just teasing, Sun. I think it's great. You and Magnus are a wonderful couple. He's completely loyal and devoted to you and he loves you with all his heart. It's obvious just by watching you together. And if you think you're ready and have really given it a lot of thought, then I say go for it."

Sunny beams. "I mean, I know we're not blood mates like you and Jareth. We're not linked by blood to stay together forever with none to tear us apart. But we're really close. I love him so much, Rayne. I don't even know how to explain it."

I watch as Jareth approaches from across the field. "It's okay, Sun," I say. "I know exactly how you feel."

"Hey, darling," Jareth says, wrapping his arms around me and pulling me close. He plants a soft kiss on my mouth and then releases me. I lean my head against his chest. I love this man. "You were great on the field," he tells me. "I thought you said you weren't cheerleading material."

"Rayne underestimates herself," Sunny says. "She always has."

"Oh whatever, pot calling kettle black," I tease back.

"Hey, don't start the party without me," Magnus says, coming up behind Sunny. She turns around and throws herself in his arms. They look so happy. I wonder if she's told him yet. He's going to be even happier.

I cuddle against Jareth. Happy like me. For once in my life I'm not thinking of the future or the past. I'm living in the present. And for the first time ever I really don't care what people think about me. I can be a Goth. I can be a cheerleader. I can be a vampire. And I can be a slayer. Whatever I want to be, I can be. And no one can tell me that those things don't mix.

"Did you rent the room?" I hear Sunny whisper to Magnus.

He nods. "It's all set, my love."

The two of them lock lips. I roll my eyes at Jareth. This constant PDA between them is a little much. I mean, Magnus is the vampire master of the coven. You'd think he'd show a little restraint when—

"Magnus?" A high-pitched female voice calling my sister's boyfriend's name makes me turn around. Crossing the field is a tall, porcelain doll–faced girl with huge eyes and a red bow mouth. She has long red hair falling down to her waist and she's wearing a slinky little black dress with platform heels.

What the hell?

Magnus and Sunny break from their make-out session and look over at the girl. I notice Magnus's normally pale face has gone ghost white.

"There you are, Magnus," the girl purrs. "I've been looking everywhere for you. I'm so glad I finally caught up with you, my love."

Sunny looks at the girl and then at Magnus, a confused look falling across her face. "What's going on?" she whispers to Magnus. "Why did she just call you her 'love'?"

Yeah, I'd like to know the same thing. "Who the hell are you?" I ask the girl, feeling protective of my sister.

The girl smiles. But not a nice smile. Her smile is loaded with venom. Like she knows something extremely amusing and will soon be using it at the expense of someone in this group.

"Who am I?" she repeats, in a voice that sounds sly and catlike. "Why don't you ask your fearless leader, Magnus?

"Magnus?" Sunny queries, looking like she's going to throw up. I don't blame her. "Who is this girl?"

Magnus swallows hard, running a hand through his hair. When he finally speaks, his voice is hoarse. "Sunny, this is Jane Johnson," he says. "She's just arrived from England. The vampire council has ruled that she is to become my Blood Mate."

To be continued . . .

JOIN THE BLOOD COVEN!

Do you want . . .

Eternal life?
Riches beyond your wildest dreams?
A hot Blood Mate to spend eternity with?

We're currently accepting applications for new Blood Coven Vampires. Sign up, take the online certification course, and get on the waiting list for your very own Blood Mate.

You'll also get to go behind the scenes, learn coven secrets, meet the vampires, watch exclusive videos, and get a sneak peek at what's coming up next for the Blood Coven Vampires.

BLOOD COVEN VAMPIRES

www.bloodcovenvampires.com

Check out all of the Blood Coven Vampire titles!

BOYS THAT BITE
STAKE THAT
GIRLS THAT GROWL

More Blood Coven Vampire action

BAD BLOOD

coming soon!